EXPECTING A ROYAL SCANDAL

BY

CAITLIN CREWS

First Published in Great Britain 2016
By Mills & Boon, an imprint of HarperCollins*Publishers*
1 London Bridge Street, London, SE1 9GF

ISBN: 978-0-263-91618-8

Our policy is to use papers that are natural, renewable and recyclable products and made from wood grown in sustainable forests. The logging and manufacturing processes conform to the legal environmental regulations of the country of origin.

Printed and bound in Spain
by CPI, Barcelona

USA TODAY bestseller and RITA® Award–nominated author **Caitlin Crews** loves writing romance. She teaches her favourite romance novels in creative writing classes at places like UCLA Extension's prestigious Writers' Programme, where she finally gets to utilise the MA and PhD in English Literature she received from the University of York in England. She currently lives in California, with her very own hero and too many pets. Visit her at caitlincrews.com.

Books by Caitlin Crews

Mills & Boon Modern Romance

Castelli's Virgin Widow
At the Count's Bidding
Undone by the Sultan's Touch
Not Just the Boss's Plaything
A Devil in Disguise
In Defiance of Duty
The Replacement Wife
Princess From the Past

The Chatsfield

Greek's Last Redemption

Scandalous Sheikh Brides

Protecting the Desert Heir
Traded to the Desert Sheikh

Vows of Convenience

His for a Price
His for Revenge

Royal and Ruthless

A Royal Without Rules

Scandal in the Spotlight

Heiress Behind the Headlines
No More Sweet Surrender

Self-Made Millionaires

Katrakis's Last Mistress

Bride on Approval

Pure Princess, Bartered Bride

Visit the Author Profile page
at millsandboon.co.uk for more titles.

To Maisey, who fixed the book once
when it had all turned a bit grim,
listened to a lot of ranting on street corners
with very broad hand gestures, and then
loved it when it was done.

CHAPTER ONE

THERE WERE SOME invitations a wise woman did not refuse.

The invitation in question tonight had been handwritten by one of the most famous men on earth on luxuriously heavy card stock and then hand-delivered to her door by a servant. The message itself had been intriguingly mysterious, asking her only to… *Meet me in Monte Carlo.*

And Brittany Hollis was many things by the ripe old age of twenty-three—including widely reviled on at least two continents thanks to her collection of strategic marriages, a reality show appearance in which she'd played the widely loathed villain and her trademark refusal to confirm or deny any and all scandalous rumors she heard about herself—but she'd always considered herself wise enough.

Too wise for her own good, in fact, or so she'd always thought. That was how an untouched virgin let herself be known across the planet as one of the most shameless women alive. Yet all the while, she stayed in control and above the snide remarks—because she, and maybe only she, knew the truth.

And no matter what names others called her, like *mercenary* when they were being polite, her ability to keep her eyes on the prize as if none of that bothered her was the best way she knew to propel her toward the tropical island paradise of her dreams.

She'd get there one day. She knew she would. She'd

spend the rest of her life in a flowing caftan sipping pitchers of mai tais with cheerful flowers in her hair, and she'd never spare a single thought for these harsh days of hustling or the cruel tabloid stories in which she was always cast as the evil villain.

Not one stray thought. Not ever again.

Brittany could hardly wait. She'd spent years sending half the money she earned back home to the family members who proclaimed her lost to the devil in public, cashed her sinner's checks in private and then shamelessly asked her for more. Again and again. Her beloved grandmother would have expected Brittany to do her part after Hurricane Katrina had wiped out what little Brittany's single mother had possessed over ten years ago, leaving them all wretched and destitute and close enough to homeless in Gulfport, Mississippi.

Brittany had done her best. Year after year, the only way she knew how, with the only weapons she possessed—her looks and her body and the wits she'd inherited straight from Grandmama, though most people assumed she was entirely witless. Her youngest half sibling was ten this year. Brittany figured that meant she had eight years left before she could suggest her family members support themselves for a change.

Though maybe she'd use stronger words.

Meanwhile, the other half of the money she made she hoarded, because one of these days she was headed for a remote Pacific Island to take up residence beneath a palm tree and the deep blue sky on a deserted white sand beach. She'd seen pictures of the archipelago of Vanuatu while still in high school, and she'd decided then and there that she needed to live in that kind of paradise. Once she made it to those perfect islands west of Fiji, she wasn't coming back to the mess of the world or her place in it.

Ever.

First, however, there was all the elegant splendor of Monaco and the man who had summoned her here to meet with him in the spectacularly iconic Monte Carlo casino where blue-blooded men like him whiled away casual evenings at gaming tables that had been specifically designed to part Europe's wealthiest from their vast, multigenerational fortunes. *To discuss a proposition that would benefit us both*, the message he'd had delivered by hand had said, though Brittany hadn't been able to think of a single thing that could possibly do that. Or anything they had in common, come to that, except a certain international notoriety—and his, unlike hers, was based on documented fact.

Documented and streamed live on the internet more than once.

Still, Brittany entered the casino that evening right on time. She'd dressed her part. Monte Carlo's achingly civilized sins were draped in the veneer of a certain old-world elegance and therefore so was Brittany. A girl liked to match. Her gown shimmered a discreet, burnished gold, sweeping from a knot on one shoulder all the way down to flirt with the gleam of her sleek heels. She was aware the dress made her look edible and expensive at once, as befitted a woman whose own mother called her a whore to her face. But it also suggested a bone-deep sophistication with every step she took, which helped a white-trash girl from Mississippi blend in with the gold-leaf and marble glory surrounding her in all directions.

Brittany was very, very good at blending.

She felt the impact of the man she'd come to Monaco to meet long before she saw him, tucked away at one of the more high risk tables in the usual throng of lackeys and admirers who cavorted about in his shadow. Even without his selection of courtiers circling him like well-heeled satellites, she would have found him without any trouble.

The whispers, the humming excitement whipping through the crowd, the not precisely subtle craning of necks to get a better view of him—it all marked him with a bright red *X*. He might as well have sent up a flare.

Then the crowd parted, and there he was, sitting at a table in a desultory manner, though his attention was on the crowd—broadcasting the fact that the man formally known as His Serene Grace the Archduke Felipe Skander Cairo of Santa Domini was so supremely wealthy and jaded he need not pay attention to his own gambling endeavors even while he was undertaking them.

Cairo Santa Domini. The exiled hereditary king of the tiny alpine country that bore his surname and the only surviving member of an august and revered family line stretching back some five hundred years. The scourge of Europe's morally compromised women, the papers liked to call him—though it was also said that a woman of impeccable reputation *became* compromised merely by standing too close to him at an otherwise staid and boring function. The living, breathing, epic scandal-causing justification for the military coup that had overturned his father's monarchy and was widely held to have assassinated the rest of his family years later, leaving only Cairo the sybaritic degenerate in their wake, like a profligate grave marker.

Largely because there was no point in targeting him, the pundits had agreed for years. He redefined *disgrace.* He did an excellent job of reminding the world why the excesses of ancient monarchies should never be tolerated, simply by continuing to draw his pampered and ill-behaved breath and cavorting about the scandal sheets like a one-man bacchanal.

Cairo Santa Domini, right there before her in the sleek, superbly fit, astonishingly handsome flesh.

His had been the name on the invitation she'd received,

of course. She'd expected she'd see him here. Yet she was somehow unprepared for him all the same.

Brittany realized she'd stopped walking and had, in fact, stopped dead in the middle of the casino. She knew better than that. Hers was a game of mirrors and sighs, of soft suggestion and affected disinterest. She did not stand about staring in shock like the yokel she hadn't been in years. That wasn't the impression she liked to give off. Yet she couldn't quite make herself move.

And then Cairo glanced over and met her gaze, bold and lazy at once, and she wasn't certain she'd ever move of her own volition again. She felt bolted to the floor—and painfully, at that.

She'd seen a thousand pictures of this man. Everyone had, and of significantly more of him than necessary. She already knew he was beautiful. Many celebrated things were from a distance, she'd found, only to prove a bit more grimy and weathered and unfortunate up close. Hollywood, for example, and many of its best-known denizens.

But not Cairo.

He had one of those full, captivating, startlingly European mouths that made her feel edgy and hollow down deep inside. That mouth of his made her imagine hot, desperate kisses in cold, unfamiliar cities bristling with baroque architecture and laden with strange pastries, when she hadn't thought about *kissing* anyone in years. He had a full head of shaggy dark hair that was obviously left mussed and careless on purpose, yet still managed to make him appear as if it had *happened* to him on the way to Monte Carlo.

And his eyes! They looked pretty enough in photographs. More than pretty. This close, a mere stone's throw across the casino floor, they were nothing short of marvelous. There was no other word to describe them. They were the color of exultantly wicked caramel and made her feel like spun sugar all the way to her toes. Her mouth watered despite herself, and she felt the heat of him in a bright blaze down deep in her belly.

This had never happened to her before. Not ever.

Brittany had been more or less immune to men since her mother's early, appalling boyfriends had raged drunkenly through their miserable trailer during Brittany's formative years. The fact she'd married three men of her own volition and for her own very practical reasons hadn't altered her opinion on the drawbacks of the male sex one bit—and not one of her husbands had affected her blood pressure like this.

Or at all, if she was honest.

It didn't make sense. She jerked her gaze from Cairo Santa Domini's too aware, slightly arrested one to take in the rest of him, not surprised to find he wore the usual uniform of all the very wealthy European men she'd ever seen out at night in this city or that, clogging up the nightclubs and restaurants and boulevard cafés. Though his version was…better.

Much better.

His dark, exquisitely tailored shirt clung to that expected glorious male torso of his that no doubt looked equally delicious framed by various Italian coasts or the yacht-choked harbors lining the French Riviera outside. His gorgeously cut dark jacket somehow made his masculine chin, with just a bit more than five o'clock shadow, seem that much more decadent and attractive. His legs, athletic and muscled and longer than most, were packed into the sort of bespoke black trousers that cost more than some people's mortgages. His shoes whispered with the quiet confidence of Milan as he stretched out his legs, continuing to lounge there, awash in his followers, as if the famed Monte Carlo tables were but a prop for a man like him.

As was she, she understood, when one of his dark brows arched high in some mixture of weary boredom and very royal command. A prop for a game she didn't yet understand—but she would. That was why she'd come.

That and she'd never before met a man who would have been an actual king, barring all that unfortunate civil unrest when he'd been a child.

Cairo crooked an imperious finger, beckoning her near, and Brittany really, truly didn't want to go to him. Every instinct inside her screamed at her to turn on her heel and run in the opposite direction. To walk all the way back up north to her efficient little flat in Paris if that was what it took.

Anything to get the hell away from him before he destroyed her.

That thought shivered over her like some kind of prophecy, bone and blood. *He will destroy you.*

She tried to shake off the feeling. She told herself she was being fanciful. Silly. Two things she'd never been in her entire life, but maybe the sight of a would-be king in a place like Monte Carlo was too much for all the broken shards of the Cinderella fantasies she knew she had rattling around inside her somewhere, scraping at her with their jagged edges when she least expected it. Making it hard to breathe in strange little moments like this one.

She started toward Cairo, affecting a faintly quizzical expression as if she hadn't recognized him. As if she'd stopped in the middle of the casino floor because she'd been uncertain where to go, not because she'd seen him and been struck by the sight. As if their gazes hadn't clashed like that, in a tangle of caramel breathlessness that was still scraping through her and making her feel almost…raw.

Brittany ignored all those inconvenient feelings, whatever the hell they were. She sauntered toward her doom, and no amount of shouting at herself to stop being so fanciful convinced her that the dissolute aristocrat who watched her approach was anything but that: her sure destruction packed into a recklessly masculine form.

"Are you Cairo Santa Domini?" she asked brightly as she drew near, letting a little more Mississippi flavor her words than usual. For dramatic effect—because people drew all sorts of conclusions about folks with drawls like the one she'd grown up using. Mostly that they were as dumb as a pile of rocks, which she'd always enjoyed using to her advantage.

As expected, her feigned inability to identify one of the most recognizable men alive was met with gasps, outraged sniffs and muttered condemnations from his entourage. Cairo's mouth, a study in carved sensuality that seemed to be wired directly into an echoing heat deep her belly, curved in appreciation.

"I regret that I am." His voice was like melted dark chocolate. Rich. Deep. Faintly, intriguingly accented, as if his use of English was an afterthought or perhaps a gift. He didn't move from his languid position, though she had the strangest notion that his decadent caramel gaze had sharpened as she approached. "But only because no one else has stepped up to take the position, no matter how I try to give it away."

"A pity." She stopped when she was *just* inside the span of his carelessly outthrust legs. She felt certain he'd appreciate the symbolism. Sure enough, that arrested, *aware* gleam in his gaze intensified. It told her she was right. And that he wasn't as bored as he was pretending to be. "Then again, no one else in all the world can boast of your indefatigable penis and its many salacious conquests, can they? What's a lost kingdom next to that?"

Brittany was aware of the ripple that deliberate slap caused all around them, ruffling the feathers of his courtiers and his more distant admirers alike. She'd meant it to do just that. And yet she couldn't seem to jerk her gaze away from the man who stood there before her—smiling, though she noticed it went nowhere near his deceptively warm eyes or the cool, calculating gleam there.

"Ms. Hollis, I presume?" he asked.

Brittany was certain he'd known her at a glance. But this was the game. So she merely nodded, all gracious condescension, as if it had been a true inquiry.

"I've been in exile most of my life," he said after a moment, his mild tone at odds with the way he was studying her. "Only the revolutionaries call me any kind of king these days. Best not to invoke their brand of fealty. It comes with toppled governments and ruined cities, generally speaking." He inclined his head, reminding her with that single, simple gesture that whatever he was now, however far he'd fallen, he'd been raised to rule. "I do hope you found your way here tonight without incident. Monte Carlo is not quite the burlesque halls of the Paris sewers—that is what we call such places in polite company, is it not? I trust you do not find yourself too far out of your accustomed, ah, *depths*."

Brittany had misjudged him. She hadn't expected a playboy royal, draped in well-dressed tarts and trailing scandal behind him wherever he roamed like some kind of acrid scent, to be anything like *sharp*. It hadn't crossed her mind that he could possibly insult her with any dexterity.

Or at all, honestly.

Some part of her shifted, deep inside, in what she told herself was grudging admiration. Nothing more.

"Water seeks its own level, I'm told," she said, and smiled all the brighter as she switched up her tactics on the fly. "And so here I am."

His impossibly carnal mouth curved again, deeper this time, and she felt it tug at her, low in her belly, where there was nothing but fire and an edgy need she didn't really understand. It seemed to intensify by the second. With every breath.

"You should, of course, feel elevated by my notice in the first place. To say nothing of my invitation." He shifted against the table at his back, propping himself up on an elbow. It only drew attention to the fact that he had to look down at her, though she stood in three-inch heels that made her nearly six feet tall. "You do not appear to be glorying in your good fortune tonight, *cara*."

"I feel very fortunate, of course," she said in an insultingly overpolite tone, as if attempting to pacify a dimwitted child. "Truly. *So* lucky."

Brittany was used to reading rooms, the better to contribute to her own tarnished legend by playing it up whenever possible. A wink here, a smile there and another rumor spread like wildfire and ended up a tabloid headline. But this was different. It wasn't only that there were no cameras allowed in this place, which made playing to them difficult. She should have been cataloguing bystander reactions to this meeting and gathering information the way she usually did—but instead, the whole of the casino seemed cast in shadow with Cairo the unlikely sun at its center, a streak of glaring brightness she found unaccountably mesmerizing.

As if he was powerful beyond measure when she knew—when everybody knew—he was at best a modern-day wastrel. He shouldn't exude anything but the latest party-boy cologne. She told herself he was a snake charmer, nothing more. Why she couldn't seem to hold on to that thought was a question she'd have to investigate in depth when she was somewhere far, far away from all this insane magnetism of his, which was far too riveting for comfort.

Cairo watched her in his oddly intent way, though every

other inch of him shouted out his pure indolence. It gave her the distinct sensation of whiplash.

"I saw your act," he said after a long, tensely glimmering moment dragged by, and Brittany found she was holding her breath. Again.

He'd been there? In the audience in that grimy little club that Europe's most pampered imagined was a walk on the wild side of their indulged little lives? Brittany couldn't believe she hadn't *felt* this intensity of his, somehow.

She hated that she felt it now. She caught herself in the act of scowling at him and softened her expression—but she was sure he'd seen it anyway.

She was certain, somehow, that Cairo Santa Domini saw a great deal more than he should.

"You have a very interesting approach to the art of the burlesque, Ms. Hollis. All that stalking about the stage, baring your teeth in such a terrifying manner at the punters. Effectively daring them to deny you their pallid offerings of a few measly bills for a glance at your frilly underthings. You'd be better off cracking a whip and dispensing with the fiction that you are at all interested in appealing to the usual fantasies, I think."

Brittany tucked her bright gold clutch beneath her arm, as languid as he was, though something in her shook at his horrifyingly accurate picture of the side gig she'd taken to make a few more scandalized headlines, and let her smile flirt with a bit of an edge.

"Are you reviewing my performance?"

"Consider it the studied reaction of a rather ardent fan of the art form."

"I don't know what's more astounding. That you sullied your aristocratic self in a burlesque club in 'the sewers of Paris,' as you call them, or that you would admit to such shocking behavior in the glare of all this fussy Monte Carlo elegance. Your desperate acolytes can hear you, you know." She leaned closer and dropped her voice to a stage whisper she was fairly certain carried all the way across the Italian border less than ten miles to the east. "You'd better be careful, Your Exiled Highness. The chandeliers themselves might shatter at the notion that a man of your known proclivities attended something so prosaic and tedious as a *nightclub*."

"I was under the impression my behavior no longer shocked a soul, or so the wearisome British papers would have me believe. In any case, do you really feel as if a return to the dance halls of your storied past are a good investment in your future? I'd thought your latest marriage was a step in a different direction. A pity about the will." That half smile of his was—she understood as it sliced through her and reminded her of the very public way her most recent husband's heirs had announced that Brittany had been excluded from the bulk his estate—an understated weapon. "I ask as a friend."

"I would be quite surprised if you truly had any friends at all." She eyed him and amped up her own smile. Polite and charming fangs. Her specialty. "But I digress. In some circles a glance at my frilly underthings is considered something of a generous gift. You're welcome."

"Ah, Ms. Hollis, let us not play these games." Something not quite a smile any longer played with that stunning mouth of his, marking him significantly more formidable than a mere *playboy*. "You did not strip, as widely advertised. You hardly performed at all, and meanwhile the chance to get a glimpse of Jean Pierre Archambault's disgraced widow in the nude was the primary attraction of the entire exercise. The whole thing was a regrettable tease."

She shrugged delicately, fully aware it made the gold fabric of her gown gleam and shimmer as if she herself was lit from within. "That must have been a novel experience for a man of your well-documented depravities."

His head tilted slightly to one side and his gaze was not particularly friendly. Somehow, this made him more beautiful. "You were a high school dropout."

Brittany knew better than to show any sort of reaction to the shift in topic. Or to what was likely meant to be a hard slap to shove her back into her place. Trouble was, she'd never much cared for her place, or she'd still be in Gulfport scraping out a miserable existence with the rest of her relatives. No, thank you.

"Did they call it something different when you failed to finish one private boarding school after the next?" she asked sweetly. His Royal Jackass wasn't the only one with access to the internet. "There were how many in a row? Six? I know the obscenely rich make their own rules, but I was under the impression your numerous expulsions meant you and I are both somehow making it through the big, bad world without a high school diploma. Maybe we'll be best friends after all."

Cairo ignored her, though she thought there was a certain appreciative gleam in those deceptively sweet-looking eyes of his. "A runaway at sixteen, in the company of your first husband. And what a prime choice he was. He was what we might call…"

He paused, as if in deference to her feelings. Or as if he'd suddenly recalled his manners. Brittany laughed.

"We called Darryl a way to get out of Gulfport, Mississippi," she replied. She let a little more twang into her voice, as emphasis. "Believe me, you make that choice when it comes along, no matter the drug-addled loser that may or may not come with it. Not the sort of choice you had to make, I imagine, while growing up coddled and adored on one of your family's numerous foreign properties."

The word *exile* called to mind something a bit more perilous than the Santa Domini royal family's collection of luxury estates; here a ranch, there an island, everywhere a sprawling penthouse in the best neighborhood of any given city. It was hard to muster up any sympathy, Brittany found, especially when her own choices had been to live wherever she could make it work or end up back in her mother's trailer.

"Your second husband was far more in the style to which you would soon become accustomed. You and he became rather well known on that dreadful television program of yours, did you not?"

"*Hollywood Hustle* ran for two seasons and is considered one of the less appalling reality shows out there," Brittany said, as if in agreement. "If we're tallying them all up."

"That's a rather low bar."

"Said the pot to the kettle." She eyed him. "Most viewers were obsessed with the heartwarming love story of Chaz and Mariella, not Carlos and me."

"The tattoo artist." Cairo didn't actually crook his fingers around the word *artist*, but it was very strongly implied. And, as Brittany recalled, deserved. "And the sad church secretary who wanted him to follow his heart and become a derivative landscape painter, or some such drivel."

"Pulse-pounding, riveting stuff," Brittany agreed dryly. "As you clearly already know, if you feel you're in a good place to judge the behavior of others despite every cautionary tale ever told about glass houses."

It had all been entirely faked, of course. Carlos had been told the gay character he'd auditioned for had already been cast, but there was an opening for a bad-girl villain and her hapless husband—as long as they were legally married. Brittany was the only woman Carlos had known who'd wanted to get out of Texas as much as he did, so the whole thing was a no-brainer. The truth was that after Darryl, Brittany didn't think too highly of the institution of marriage anyway. She and Carlos had been together long enough to get reality-show famous—which wasn't really famous at all, despite what so many people in her family seemed to think—and then, when the show's ratings started to fade and their name recognition went with them, Brittany had dramatically "left" Carlos for Jean Pierre, so Carlos could complain about it in the tabloids and land himself a new gig.

But to the greater public, of course, she was that low-class slut who had ruined a poor, sweet, good man. A tale as old as time, blah blah blah.

She raised her brows at Cairo Santa Domini now. "I wouldn't have pegged you for a fan of the show. Or any reality show, for that matter. I thought inhabitants of your social strata wafted about pretending to read Proust."

"I spend a lot of my time on airplanes, not in glass houses and very rarely with Proust," Cairo replied, a glint in the caramel depths of his gaze as he waved a careless hand. "Your show was such a gripping drama, was it not? You, the heartless stripper who wouldn't give up your tawdry dancing for the good of your marriage. Carlos, the loving husband who tried so desperately to stay true to you despite the way you betrayed him on those poles every night. The path of true love, et cetera."

Brittany felt the flash of her own smile as she aimed it at him, and concentrated on making it brighter. Bolder. It was amazing what people failed to see in the glare of a great smile.

"I'm a terrible person," she agreed merrily. "If a television show says so, it must be true. Speaking of which, didn't I see you featured on one of those tabloid programs just last week? Something about a hapless heiress, a weekend in the Maldives and the corrosive nature of your company?"

"Remind me," Cairo murmured, sounding somewhat less amused—she was almost certain. "Were you still married to Carlos when you met Jean Pierre?"

Brittany laughed. A sparkling, effortless, absolutely false laugh. "You appear to be confusing my résumé with yours."

"And speaking of Jean Pierre, may he rest in peace, what was it that drew you together? He, the elderly man confined to a wheelchair with a scant few months to live. You…"

Cairo let his gaze travel over her form, as hot and buttery as a touch. He didn't finish that sentence.

"We had a shared interest in applied sciences, of course," Brittany replied, deadpan and dry. "What else?"

"An interest that his children did not share, given they wasted no time in ejecting you from the old man's chateau the moment he died and then crowing about it to the press. A shame."

"Your invitation didn't mention that we'd be playing biography games," Brittany said brightly, as if it didn't bother her in the least to be so publically eviscerated. "I feel so woefully underprepared. Let's see." She held her bag beneath her elbow and ticked things off on her fingers. "Royal blood. No throne. Always naked. Eight thousand women. So many sex tapes. So scandalous the word no longer really applies because it's really more, 'there's Cairo Santa Domini somewhere he shouldn't be with someone he shouldn't have touched and blurred out bits in a national newspaper. La la la, must be Tuesday.'"

"Ms. Hollis," Cairo said in that drawling way only extremely upper-crust people could manage to make sound so condescending. When it was only her name. He reached over as if nothing had ever been more inevitable and then he traced a very lazy, very delicate path from the gold knot at her shoulder to the very top of that shadow between her breasts. Sensation detonated inside of her. She flashed white hot. She saw red. She *felt* him, everywhere, and that voice of his, too, all dark chocolate and stupendously bad decisions melted into something that shivered through her, dessert and desire and destruction all at once. "You flatter me."

Brittany didn't like the way her heart catapulted itself against the wall of her chest. She didn't like the way her skin prickled, hot and cold, as if she was sunburned from so small and meaningless a touch. Since when had she reacted at all to a man? No matter what he did?

She didn't like the fact that she'd completely lost sight of the fact that they were in public, even if the public in question was mostly his circle of pseudosubjects she knew trotted around with him everywhere he went—or that all she'd really seen since she walked in here was Cairo. As if she'd come here to compete for his attention, like one of his usual horde of panting women.

She liked that part least of all, and she didn't care to ask herself why that was. It didn't matter. None of what had happened here mattered. This spectacularly messy and inappropriate man wasn't in any way a part of her grand plan, and would do nothing but delay her dreams of a getaway to her solitary tropical island paradise in Vanuatu. He had that kind of total disaster written all over him, and too much exposure to him made her worry it was written on her, too. She'd accepted his invitation because she was curious and he was Cairo Santa Domini, and now she knew.

He was her ruin made flesh. Nothing less than that. At least she knew it now, she told herself. That meant she had the chance to avoid it. To avoid *him.*

"Your Almost Highness," she breathed, in exaggerated shock.

She wanted to snatch his lazy finger away from her

overheated skin, which was why she leaned into it instead. His finger slipped into the valley between her breasts, *just there* beneath the edge of her angled bodice, but neither one of them looked down to see what both of them could feel. Their gazes were locked together, tangled up hot and a little bit wild, and Brittany was slightly mollified to see she wasn't the only one affected by…whatever the hell this was. She raised her voice so they could hear her everywhere in Monaco, the trashy American that she was, every inch of her offensive to each and every highbrow European eye that tried its best not to see her.

But Brittany wasn't any good at being invisible. "Are you *flirting* with me?"

CHAPTER TWO

A SHORT WHILE LATER, Cairo stood with his back to the disconcerting American, his brooding gaze fixed on the seductive glitter of Monaco's harbor out there in the sweet summer dark. The night pressed in on the glass windows of his penthouse suite the way that woman seemed to hammer against his composure, even when all she was doing was sitting quietly on his sofa. He could see her reflection in the glass and it irritated him that she looked so calm while he had to fight to collect himself.

That he had to do any such thing was nothing short of extraordinary for a man who was alive today precisely because he could so expertly manage himself in all situations.

But then, nothing tonight was going according to plan.

Brittany Hollis wasn't at all what he'd expected. When he'd watched that cringe-worthy television program of hers she'd been all plumped-up breasts and an endless Southern drawl, punctuated with supple flips and melting slides on the nearest stripper pole. All the advance research he'd done on her before selecting her for the dubious honor of his proposal had suggested she might possess the particular cunning native to the sort of women whose life revolved around strategic relationships with much wealthier men, but he hadn't expected any great intellect.

Cairo had been delighted at the prospect that she'd be exactly as gauche as her tawdry history suggested she was.

Someone capable of injecting the embarrassing spectacle of her risqué burlesque appearances into everyday life and making certain the whole world found her deeply embarrassing and epically shameless at all times.

The perfect woman for him, in other words. A man so famously without honor or country deserved a shameful match, he'd told himself bitterly the night he'd seen her dance. Brittany Hollis seemed crafted to order.

Instead, the woman who had walked up to him tonight was a vision, from the pale copper fire of her hair to the hint of hot steel in her dark hazel eyes, and there wasn't a single thing the least bit dumb or plastic about her. He didn't understand it. Meeting her gaze had been like being thrown from the saddle of a very large horse and having to lie there on the hard ground for a few excruciating moments, wondering with no little panic if he'd ever draw breath to fill his lungs again.

He still didn't know the answer to that.

His long-term head of security, Ricardo, who'd suggested this tabloid sensation of a woman in the first place, had a lot to answer for. But here, now, Cairo had to navigate what he'd expected to be a very straightforward business conversation despite the fact he felt so…unsettled.

"Have you lured me back to your hotel suite to show me your etchings, Your Usually Far More Naked Grace?" Brittany's voice was so dry it swept over him like a brush fire, igniting a longing in him he'd never imagined he'd feel for anyone or anything aside from his lost kingdom and its people. He didn't understand what this was—what was happening to him, when he'd felt absolutely nothing since the day he'd lost his family and had understood what waited for him if he wasn't careful. What General Estes, the self-appointed Grand Regent of Santa Domini, had made clear was Cairo's destiny if he ever so much as glanced longingly at the throne that should have been his.

"What a dream come true. I've always wanted to join such a vast and well-populated parade of royal paramours."

That the girl was perfect for his purposes wasn't in doubt, dry tone or not.

Cairo had known it the moment Ricardo had handed him her picture. Even before Ricardo had told him anything about the pretty redhead who wore so little and stared into the camera with so much distance and mystery in her dark eyes. He'd felt something scratch at him, and he'd told himself that was reason enough to conceal himself and sneak into one of her scandalous performances in Paris. He'd been far more intrigued than he should have been as he'd watched her command the stage, challenging the audience with every sinuous move of her famously lithe and supple figure.

He'd sent one of his aides with his invitation and he'd continued interviewing the other candidates for his very special position, but his heart wasn't in it once he'd seen Brittany. And that was before he'd read all the unsavory details of her life story, which, of course, rendered her an utterly appalling if not outright ruinous choice for a man some people still dreamed would be king one day. General Estes might have routed Cairo's father from the throne of Santa Domini when Cairo was still a small child, but the passing of time only ever seemed to make the loyalists more shrill and focused. And that made no one safe—neither Cairo nor the Santa Dominian people, who didn't deserve another bloody coup in a thirty-year span, much less the empty-headed playboy prince Cairo played for the papers as its figurehead.

Besides, Cairo knew what the loyalists refused to see—there was nothing good in him. He'd seen to that. There was only shame and darkness and more of the same. Play a role long enough and it ate a man alive. The desperate American stripper who'd made an international game out of her shameless gold digging was an inspired choice to make certain that even if no one listened to Cairo about who he'd become, no coup could ever happen and his people would be spared a broken, damaged king.

And then she'd walked up to him in a dress of spun gold and pretended not to know him, and he'd forgotten he'd ever so much as considered another woman for this role at all.

"Was it a lure?" he asked now. He turned to see her rolling her glass of wine between her palms, an action he shouldn't have found even remotely erotic. And yet... "I asked you to accompany me to my hotel suite and you agreed. A lure is rather less straightforward."

"If you say so, Your Semantic Highness."

Cairo had expected to find her attractive. He'd expected a hint of the usual fire deep within him and the lick of it in his sex, because he was a man, after all. Despite what he needed to do here. He'd been less prepared for the sheer wallop of her. Of how the sight of her made his breath a complication in his chest.

And he certainly hadn't imagined she'd be...entertaining.

The pictures and even the stage hadn't done her any justice at all, and the tidy little marriage of convenience he'd imagined shifted and re-formed in his head the longer he looked at her. Cairo knew he should call it off. The last thing he needed in his life was one more situation he couldn't control, and the blazing thing raging inside of him now was the very definition of uncontrollable.

And *she* was something more than a gorgeous redhead who'd looked edible in a down-market burlesque ensemble, or even a former American television star in a shiny dress that made her look far more sophisticated than she should have been. Brittany Hollis should have been little more than a jumped-up tart. Laughable in the midst of so much old-world splendor here in Monaco.

But instead, she was fascinating.

Cairo was finding it exceedingly difficult to keep his cool, which had never happened to him before in all the years since he'd lost his family. He hardly knew whether to give in to the sensation, unleashing God knew what manner of hell upon himself, or view it as an assault. Both, perhaps.

"Is this the part where we stare at each other for ages?" Brittany asked from her position on the crisp white sofa where she perched with all the boneless elegance of a pampered cat. "I had no idea royal intrigue was so tedious."

It was time to handle this. To handle himself, for God's sake. This wasn't about *him*, after all, or whatever odd need he felt licking at him, tempting him to forget the dark truths about himself in earnest for the first time in some twenty years.

"Of course it's tedious," he said, drawing himself up to his full height. He brushed a nonexistent speck of lint from one sleeve. "That's why kings are forced to start wars or institute terror regimes and inquisitions, you understand. To relieve the boredom."

"And your family was drummed out of your country. I can't think why."

Cairo had long since ceased to allow himself to feel anything at all when it came to his lost kingdom and the often vicious comments people made about it to his face. He'd made an art out of seeming not to care about his birthright, his blood, his people. He'd locked it all up and shoved it deep inside, where none of it could slip out and torture him any longer, much less trip him up in the glare of the public eye.

No stray memories of graceful white walls cluttered with priceless art, the dizzy blue sky outside his window in that particular bright shade he'd never seen replicated anywhere else, the murmur of the mountain winds against the fortified walls of his childhood bedroom in the castle heights. No recollections of the night they'd all been spirited away in the dark before General Estes could get his butcher's hands on them, hidden in the back of a loyalist's truck across the sharp spine of the snowcapped mountains that ringed the capital city, never to return.

He didn't let himself think of his father's roar of laughter or his mother's soft hands, lost forever. He never permitted himself any stray thoughts about his younger sister, Magdalena, a bright and gleaming little girl snatched away so easily and so unfairly.

He didn't have the slightest idea why the usual barbed comments from yet another stranger should lodge in him tonight like a mortal blow, as if the fact this woman had surprised him meant she could slip beneath his defenses, too. No one could do that. Not if he didn't let them.

And he was well aware that even if he'd wanted someone close to him, to that tarnished thing inside of him he called his soul, he couldn't allow it to happen. He couldn't let anyone close to him or they'd be rendered so much more collateral damage. One more weapon the general would find a way to use against Cairo and then destroy.

Why was Brittany Hollis making him consider such things?

He studied her. Her coppery hair was caught up in a complicated twist, catching the light as she moved. Her neck was long and elegant, and made him long for a taste of her. More than a taste. Her skin looked as if it was dusted a fainter gold than the dress she wore, which on any other woman might have been a trick of cosmetics, but on this one, he thought, was actually *her.* She was far prettier than her photographs and infinitely more captivating than her coarse appearances on that stupid show. She was all impossibly long legs, those lovely curves shimmering beneath the expert cling of the gown and that enticing intelligence simmering there in her dark eyes.

That same thing scratched at him, the way it had in Paris when Ricardo had given him her picture, and he knew better than to let it. This was already a mess. A problem, and he had enough of those already. He needed a clear path and a solution, or what was the point of this game? He might as well hand himself over to the general for the execution that had already been meted out to the rest of his bloodline and call it a day.

Some part of him—a part that grew larger all the time—wished he'd done just that, years ago. Some part of him wished he'd been in that car with the rest of his family when it had been run off the road. Some part of him wished he'd never lived long enough to make these choices.

But that was nothing but craven self-pity. The least of his sins, but a sin nonetheless.

"You are very pretty," he told her now. Sternly.

"I would thank you, but somehow I doubt it was a compliment."

"It is surprising. I expected you to be attractive, of course, in the way all women of your particular profession are." He waved a hand.

She smiled, managing to convey an icy disdain that would do a royal proud. "My profession?"

Cairo shrugged. "Dancer. Television personality. Expensive trophy wife, ever open to the appropriate upgrades. Whatever you call yourself."

Her smile took on that edge that fascinated him, but she didn't look away.

"I do like an upgrade." She fingered the rim of her glass and he remembered the feel of her skin under his hand, hot and soft at once. Touching her had been a serious miscalculation, he was aware. One that pounded in him still, kicking up dark yearnings and desperate longings he knew he needed to ignore. "Are you going to tell me why I'm here?"

"No insulting version of my title this time? I'm wounded."

"I find my creativity wanes along with my interest." She leaned forward and set her glass down on the table before her with a decisive *click*. "Monte Carlo is wasted on me, I'm afraid, as I'm not much of a gambler." Her smile didn't reach her eyes. "I prefer the comfort of a sure thing. And I loathe being bored."

"Is this what boredom looks like on you? My mistake. I rather thought you looked a bit…flushed."

"I find myself ever so slightly nauseated." He knew she was lying. The glitter in her bright eyes told him so, if he'd had the slightest doubt. "I can't think why."

He thrust his hands into the pockets of his trousers. "Perhaps you dislike penthouses with extraordinary views." He smiled. "The coast or me. Take your pick. Both views, and I say this with no false modesty at all, are stunning."

"Maybe I dislike spoiled rich men who waste my time and think far too highly of their overexposed charms." The edge to her smile and that glittering thing in her gaze grew harder. Hotter. "I've seen it all in the pages of every tabloid magazine every week for the last twenty years. It's about as thrilling as oatmeal."

"I must have misheard you. I thought you compared me to a revoltingly warm and cloying breakfast cereal."

"The similarities are striking."

"A man with less confidence than I have—and no access to a mirror—might find that hurtful, Ms. Hollis."

"I feel certain you find whatever you need in all the reflective surfaces available to you." She eyed him. "I suppose that almost qualifies as a skill. But while that confirms my opinion of your conceit, it doesn't tell me what I'm doing here."

Cairo hadn't decided precisely how he would do this. Somewhere in his murky, battered soul he'd imagined this might prove a rare opportunity to be honest. Or as near enough to honest as he was capable of being, anyway. He'd imagined that might make purchasing a wife to ward off a revolution a little less seedy and sad, no matter his reasons. A little self-deprecating humor and a few hard truths, he'd imagined, and the whole thing would be easily sorted.

But he hadn't expected to want her this badly.

"I have a proposition for you," he forced himself to say, before he made the unfortunate decision to simply seduce her instead and see what happened. He already knew what would happen—didn't he?—and the pleasures of the moment couldn't outweigh the realities of the future bearing down on him. He knew that.

He couldn't believe he was even considering it.

"I'd say I'm flattered," Brittany was saying coolly, "but I'm not. I'm not interested in being any man's mistress. And not to put too fine a point on it, but your charms are a bit…" She raised her brows. "Overused."

He blinked, and took his time with it. "I beg your pardon. Did you just call me a whore?"

"I'd never use that word," Brittany demurred, and though her voice was smooth he was sure there was something edgy and sharp lurking just beneath it. "But the phrase *rode hard and put away wet* comes to mind." She waved a hand at him. "It's all a bit boring, if I'm honest."

"Do not kid yourself, Ms. Hollis," Cairo advised her quietly. "I've had a lot of sex with a great many partners, it's true."

"That's a bit like the ocean confessing it's slightly damp."

He smiled. “The media coverage of my sex life might indeed be boring. I wouldn’t know as I make a point never to follow it. But the act itself? Never.”

“You’d be the last to know, of course. Even a man as conceited as you are must realize that.”

“I suppose the first hundred or so could simply be interested in my dramatic personal history,” Cairo said, as if considering her point, though he kept his gaze trained on the increasing color high up on her cheeks. *Interesting.* “And the second two hundred could be in it for my personal wealth. But *all* of them? The law of averages suggests not *all* of them would come apart like that, screaming and wailing and crying beneath me. The same reasoning applies if you suggest they were faking it. Some, I imagine, because there are always some. But all?”

“I’m sure you saw whatever it is you wanted to see.” He could have sworn there was a huskiness in her voice and a deeper shade to the red of her cheeks, and he didn’t care what she said. He knew passion when he saw it. She was as affected as he was. “Ninety times a day, or whatever the horrifying number is. The mind boggles.”

Cairo was no saint, by design or inclination. But he was also not quite the epic sinner he’d played all his life. And in all the years he’d performed his role in the circus that was his life, he’d never felt the slightest urge to tell a woman that. What the hell was happening to him tonight?

“I’m only good at one thing,” he told her, the way he’d have told anyone else. He pretended he couldn’t hear the intensity in his own voice. He pretended he had no idea how little in control of himself he was just then. “And as it happens, I’m very, very good at it.”

She swallowed, which he shouldn’t have found even remotely fascinating, no matter how elegant her neck. “Is that your proposition? My answer is an emphatic no, as I said. But also, your pitch needs some work.”

"That I'm an excellent lover is a fact, not a pitch," Cairo said with a small shrug. He found he was enjoying himself, which was almost as unusual as the claws of need that still raked through him. "The proposition is far less exciting, I'm afraid. I'm not in the market for a mistress, Ms. Hollis. Why would I bother with such a confining arrangement? I rarely meet a woman who wouldn't do anything I ask for free, no need to provide room, board or baubles on demand."

"I'm overcome by the romance of it all."

"Then this will delight you." Cairo eyed her, a column of gold tipped in all that sweet copper he wanted to bury his hands in, and he found his blood was pumping much too hard through his body then, as if he was out on a long, hard run in a harsh winter. He ignored it. "I find myself in need of a wife. I've been considering a number of candidates for the position, but you are far and away my first choice."

He expected her to say something scathing. Perhaps let out a scandalized laugh. He even braced himself for the lash of it, and damned if he didn't enjoy the anticipation of that, too. But she only considered him for a moment, her dark hazel gaze unreadable, and he found he had no idea what she might say.

That, like everything else with this woman, was a new experience. He told himself he hated it. Because he should have. He needed an employee of sorts, at minimum. A partner if at all possible. What he did not need was any more trouble, and Brittany Hollis had that stamped deep on every inch of her lovely skin.

God knew he had enough trouble. It lived inside him. It was his world.

"Who's your second choice?" she asked when the silence had drawn out almost too long.

"My second choice?"

Brittany didn't *quite* roll her eyes. "I can hardly determine whether to be insulted or complimented if I don't know the field, can I?"

Cairo named a famously orphaned Italian socialite, primarily well-known for her bouts of sulky nudity on board the superyachts of her questionable Russian oligarch boyfriends.

Brittany sighed. "Insulted it is."

"She's a far second, if that helps. Far too much work for too little return."

This surprising American, who he'd expected would fall at his feet in an instant and who cared if that was as much about his credit line and his title as the charms she'd called *overused* to his face, only gazed at him a moment, her dark eyes narrow. He thought he could *see* her thinking and he didn't understand why or how he could find that the sexiest thing he'd seen in years. It was that glint in her hazel gaze. It was moving through him like something alcoholic.

"You don't actually want to get married, then. You want to inflict your wife on someone—the world, perhaps? As any girl would be, I'm of course delighted to be considered an infliction. It's all my dearest fairy-tale fantasies made real, thank you."

He couldn't help but smile at her dry tone, though the curve of his own mouth felt as hard as granite. "I'm sorry, did you expect protestations of love? I could do that, if you like. You can even believe them, if it helps. But the offer is for a job. A position. Not a romantic interlude."

Those too-dark eyes held his for a moment that stretched on a little too long for comfort. Then even longer. And Cairo had never wanted to read another person's mind as much as he did then.

"I feel certain there's a middle ground." She stood, running an unnecessary hand over the sleek fall of her gown as she did, and Cairo found he wanted her with a raw fervor that shook through him, making him a total stranger to himself. Making him a traitor to his cause. Making her nothing less than a calamity—which only made the wanting worse. "I'd suggest you find it before you approach the socialite. I've heard she bites."

And then Brittany Hollis—so far beneath him that she should have been prostrate with gratitude at his attention to her and appreciative of the faintest bare crumb of his interest—actually turned on her heel, showed him her back as if he really did bore her silly and walked out.

Halfway through her burlesque performance a few nights later, Brittany felt an electric ripple go through the crowd. And seconds later, through her.

She told herself she was imagining things as she strode across the stage to the pulsing beat, but she knew better. She knew that feeling, like being lit on fire and forced to stand still in the crackling flames. That was exactly how she'd felt in Monte Carlo, burnt to a crisp where she stood on the casino floor.

Brittany concentrated on the pounding music and on the lazy choreography she could perform by rote. Something she was even happier about than usual, because she could hardly pay attention to this kick or that shimmy when she could *feel* Cairo's presence like some kind of tsunami, washing through the club. She didn't have to squint to see him past the swirling lights the club owner went a little overboard with during her number. She didn't have to try to make out his features as he moved through the dark.

She could track him by the murmur and shift in the crowd as they swiveled around in their chairs to watch him pass. She could feel the way that deceptively lush gaze of his settled on her and stayed there. It was a little too much like the dreams she kept having, the ones that spun out different, far more erotic endings to that night in his hotel suite in Monaco—when she'd never wanted a man's touch in her life. She felt that same great rush of complicated, messy feelings, the way she did each time she woke up with her heart pounding and her breath tangled in her throat, her body too warm and somehow no longer her own.

And suddenly the crimson corset she wore seemed a good deal tighter across her breasts and the black lace choker at her neck lived up to its name with a vengeance. She was aware of the creamy expanse of her upper thighs that peeked out above her garters, and the way the sleek sleeves that hooked over her pointer fingers, but covered her forearms to her elbows, left her upper arms bare. The frilly, puffy shrug she wore that made her look one step away from steampunk seemed insubstantial, suddenly, and she understood what Cairo had called "the art of the burlesque" in a different way than she ever had before.

Brittany didn't want to investigate that—much less the great swirl of *feelings* that nearly knocked her sideways on the main stage. She simply danced toward it.

Toward him.

Toward Cairo as he moved to the reserved table that had been kept empty right there in the front all night, so there was no pretending she didn't see him when—at last—he stopped showing off for the goggle-eyed audience and settled himself in the chair closest to the stage as if he owned this place and everything in it. The dancers before him, most of all.

It was Brittany's turn then, and she took it.

He'd been right about her previous performances. She'd been phoning it in, having promised the club owner eight weeks of shows and not caring too much about it after the first rash of appalled tabloid headlines. Tonight, however, seven weeks into her run, it turned out she had something to prove.

To him, a little voice clarified.

She didn't ask herself what she was doing, just as she didn't question why the things he'd said to her and the proposition he'd made—far less offensive than most of the things she'd been called and a huge percentage of the offers she'd fielded in her time—had needled her ever since. Brittany simply danced.

For him, something inside her whispered.

Up there on the stage, dressed in bright red, frilly almost underthings, she didn't care if he knew it. She danced as if there was no one else in the room. She danced as if they had long been lovers, a cheap, trashy girl like her and a man who could have had a throne. She danced as if this whole cavernous club was a king's harem, and she had no goal in all the world but to please him.

Because he wasn't the only one who was good at what he did.

The truth was, the only thing in her life Brittany had ever really loved besides her grandmother was dancing. It had gotten lost there, in the brutal reality of her first marriage and the Hollywood fakery of her second. She'd turned it into pole tricks and barely there G-strings and all manner of mugging for the camera to pay her bills. She'd used it to inform the way she moved and breathed and insinuated herself in the path of tabloid reporters and future husbands alike. But deep down inside of her was the sheer love of movement and music and the fusion of the two that, once upon a time, had been her only way out of the grim realities of her life in Mississippi.

Brittany drew on all of that now.

She danced to him, for him. She wound herself around the poles and she strutted across the stage, until she felt as if she was flying. She'd gone completely electric by the time she skidded to her dramatic finish—sliding across the stage on her knees with her hands stretched out in front of her, ending up face-to-face with Cairo as the music ended.

And it was as if she'd tipped off the side of the world, straight into that hot caramel gaze of his. Spun sugar and hot sex.

The crowd made noise all around them. She could hear the DJ on the microphone as if from a great distance. She was aware of the stage beneath her knees and the hands she'd stretched out toward Cairo in some or other form of supplication—

All feigned, she reminded herself sternly. All part of her performance, no matter how oddly right and real it felt to be stretched out before Cairo Santa Domini as if he was the only man in the whole club. Or perhaps the world.

As if nothing could possibly matter but him.

That should have set off all kinds of alarms inside of her, especially when she knew exactly what he wanted from her and, more than that, what he must think of her in the first place to offer it. That it was what she'd gone to excessive lengths to make sure everyone already thought of her didn't seem to matter.

The world didn't hurt her feelings any longer. Yet somehow, Cairo had.

Did you expect protestations of love? he'd asked, his voice scathingly amused. It had cut her. Deep.

She told herself she didn't know why.

Yet here, now, at the end of a silly dance in a stupid costume that had never affected her one bit before, all Brittany could see was Cairo. Caramel eyes burning bright and hot and that intoxicating mouth set to something far too edgy for her peace of mind. She could feel it move in her, from the breasts that wanted to break free of her constricting corset, to that low, odd ache in her belly that she tried her hardest to ignore.

"That was perfectly adequate," Cairo said, his voice pitched to slice through the clamor pressing in around them, his mouth set in a little crook.

It went straight through her all over again, little as she wanted to admit it.

Brittany shifted, rolling back so she kneeled upright on the stage above him, no longer at eye level. That felt safer, no matter that her heart clapped wildly against her ribs. She forced herself to gaze down at him coolly. Challenging and wholly unbothered, as he'd accused her of being in Monte Carlo. How she wished it was true, the way it always had been before, with every man she'd ever met in all her life. Except this one.

"Are you slumming, Your Most Graceless?" She raised her brows as she swung her legs around in front of her and then slid from the stage to stand before the chair where, once again, he lounged as if he'd presented himself for a study in aristocratic laziness. "Maybe you don't know the rules this far from the golden embrace of the Champs-Élysées. If you want a private chat, you need to pay for the privilege."

He didn't quite smile. And his eyes seemed to darken the more his mouth curved.

"Let me hasten to assure you I know my way around establishments of ill repute." He tilted his head to one side and that gaze of his went very nearly lethal. She felt it like his hand wrapped tight around her throat, rendering her choker superfluous. Or maybe that was her heart, pounding so hard she thought it might tip her over. He indicated his lap with a jerk of his chin, never shifting his gaze from hers. "Come, Brittany. Show me what you've got. I promise, I can pay."

CHAPTER THREE

HER NAME IN Cairo's decadent mouth, instead of that drawled *Ms. Hollis*, was like a lick against the hottest, sweetest part of her. It jolted through her, lightning need and the same dancing fire, making her melt. Everywhere.

Brittany couldn't seem to jerk her gaze away from his, and even knowing how dangerous that was didn't make it any easier. Her heart was a hammer against every pulse point, slamming into her again and again, but she made herself smile as she shifted position into something more pinup worthy, as was expected of a woman wearing as little as she was.

She told herself it was the game. What the costume demanded.

And so what if she'd never given an audience member the time of day after a performance before? *This is different*, she told herself, with starch. *This is our own little war, him and me, and I'll win it.*

"Was I unclear in Monaco?" she asked him. She was aware that they were attracting all kinds of stares as the music cued up the next act, but she couldn't bring herself to pay attention to that the way she knew she should. She couldn't break away from the tractor beam of his arrogant gaze long enough to read the room and react accordingly, and she didn't want to think about the implications of the situation. "I thought my walking off without a backward glance was a fairly straightforward message."

"I assumed that was a ploy," he replied in that same deceptively mild way of his that really shouldn't tear through her the way it did, making her feel hollow and needy and too many other raw things to name. "I thought I'd come here and speak to you in the language you understand."

"Rather than in Pompous Ass, the language of rich men? Don't worry, I'm fluent."

He didn't answer that directly. Still holding her gaze with his, he reached into the inside pocket of the sleek coat he wore and pulled out a leather billfold fat with euros. Very, very fat. He didn't so much as glance at it, he simply peeled a purple note from inside and slapped it on the table. Then another. And another.

"You appear to be suggesting I'm motivated by five-hundred euro notes," Brittany said. Through her teeth. "Surely not."

Cairo didn't say a word. He merely added another note to the pile. Then another. One after the next.

"I'm sure I'm mistaken," she bit out, as the pile continued to grow. "You can't possibly be calling me a prostitute, can you?"

He didn't quite laugh. Not quite.

"Of course not," he replied, in a scrupulously innocent voice that made the lie of it feel like a slap. "Your prices are much higher and you require legal vows, if your matrimonial history is any guide. Hardly a rendezvous in a back alley, is it?"

"True," Brittany replied, her voice a different sort of slap that her palms itched to replicate against that dark-shadowed jaw of his. "But I have no intention or interest in making vows of any kind with you."

That sharp smile of his edged over into something feral.

"So you say." He threw another few bills onto the tabletop, carelessly and insultingly. Deliberately so, she imagined. "Then a lap dance it is."

Brittany jerked her attention away from him for a moment to see the club owner over by the bar, furiously gesturing for her to sit down. To stop blocking access to the stage, she realized, now that the next act had started. And it was simple, of course. She should merely walk away from Cairo again the way she'd done once already. She should pretend she'd never met him. She wanted nothing more than to do exactly that.

So she had no idea why instead, she settled herself on the arm of his chair and gazed down into his face as if she really was the hardened stripper she'd played on TV instead of the innocent sometimes even she forgot she really was.

"I don't give lap dances," she told him loftily, pretending she hadn't surrendered something critical in sitting down like this. As if that blaze in his caramel gaze didn't show sheer male victory and something edgier besides. As if she didn't recognize she'd lost what little ground she'd gained by denying him in Monaco. "Though I'm happy to take your money, of course. You appear to have far too much of it."

Cairo shrugged as if it was nothing to him, the thousands of euros in a purple pile on the table. What were mere thousands to a man who had untold billions in property alone?

"All I want is a dance," he told her, and he was so much closer now than he had been in Monaco. Too close.

The arms of the seats were made deliberately wide and comfortable, all the better for the girls to perch upon, so she wasn't touching him—because Brittany didn't do *touching.* Especially not with men. And she told herself she didn't recognize that craving in her for what it was, elemental and obvious, so close to that magnificent body of his as he lounged there that she could feel the heat he generated in the space between them.

Then he made everything that much more mad and wild when he reached over and started to trace a lazy little pattern against the skin of the thigh nearest him, right at the top of her stocking and below the ruffled red-and-black underwear she wore.

Back and forth. Back and forth.

She wanted to leap up. She wanted to slap his hand away. She wanted to slap *him* like the offended virgin she actually was, but she didn't dare give herself away like that. And the more she sat there and let Cairo touch her, the more she seemed to forget why allowing this to happen was such a terrible idea.

They both watched his idle finger for a while. Maybe entire years—decades—while inside, everything Brittany had ever been and everything she knew about herself crumbled into dust and shivered away until there was nothing left of her but that pulsing heat between her legs.

Her worst fear come true.

But she still didn't move.

"Or perhaps you prefer a private room after all," Cairo said, the low rumble of his insinuating voice adding to the spell he cast with that impossibly elegant finger against her thigh rather than breaking it. "Is this how you upsell the punters, Ms. Hollis?"

Brittany jerked her attention away from that mesmerizing, addictive pattern he kept drawing against her flesh, and told herself it was the insult of what he'd said—not that he'd reverted back to *Ms. Hollis*. But his gaze was worse than his touch. Too bright, too hot.

And the last thing in the world she wanted was to be locked away in some private room with this man. She knew she couldn't trust him, of course. He'd made the fact he couldn't be trusted something that practically required a celebration. But she was suddenly so much more afraid she couldn't trust herself.

"I think not," she managed to say, but she didn't sound like herself. She sounded as thrown as she felt.

Something flashed over his famous, beautiful face. She felt it echo inside of her like a roll of thunder and then, suddenly, he wasn't lounging there idly any longer. She hardly saw him move. All she knew was that one moment she sat there on the arm of his chair, barely clinging to the pretense of some civility and everything she'd ever known about herself, and the next she was sprawled across his lap.

She wanted to scream. To fight. She wanted that more than anything—so she had no idea why she simply melted against him, as if she'd lost all control of the body that had done her bidding the whole of her life.

She had never been tempted, by anyone. She had never *melted*, ever.

Cairo was hard beneath her, hot and perfect, his legs so strong they marked his studied laziness as yet another lie. His arms closed around her, holding her against his sculpted chest and she couldn't seem to *breathe.* She couldn't breathe and she couldn't speak and she had no idea why she was letting any of this happen.

Especially when he bent and brought his face so close to hers.

So. Damned. Close.

"You'd better brace yourself," she managed to tell him, though she sounded far more thrown by this than she would have liked. And still it was nowhere near as thrown as she *felt.* "The security guards take a dim view of unauthorized touching in the main room."

"When will you learn that the rules do not apply to me?" Cairo's mouth was a breath away from hers, and the thick, glossy fall of his shaggy hair brushed her cheek as he bent over her, his dark eyes gleaming. "And that sooner or later, all mere mortals do exactly as I ask?"

"I'm not giving you a lap dance," she told him, though

her heart was drumming at her again, so hard she was glad she wore that lace choker so there was no chance he could see it there in the hollow of her throat. “And I’m not marrying you, either. I don’t even like you.”

“What the hell does that have to do with anything?” Cairo muttered, sounding less like a king and more like a man than she’d heard him yet. “This has nothing to do with *like.*”

And then he yanked her mouth to his.

He never should have tasted her.

It was a terrible mistake in a night brimming with too many of them already. He should not have come to this crass place in a temper. He should not have indulged in that temper in the first place, for that matter. He should have laughed at the absurdity of a woman of so little breeding declining his offer to better herself so spectacularly and then moved on. Hell, he should have forgotten she existed at all the moment the door of his suite in Monaco had shut behind her.

Instead, he’d brooded over it. Over her.

“The world is full of inappropriate women, Sire,” Ricardo had pointed out earlier this evening. “It’s one of its few charms.”

“It seems I require a particular blend of inappropriate and interesting,” Cairo had replied, having spent the days since Monaco convincing himself of precisely that. It wasn’t that only Brittany Hollis would do. It wasn’t that he was unused to rejection. Both of those things were true. But what mattered more, he’d assured himself, was that his very *requirements* had changed. “If there are more who fit the bill, by all means, present them to me.”

But Ricardo had wisely said nothing, and here Cairo was.

And this inarguably terrible mistake he was making

felt like sweet, hot glory and all manner of dark and lovely sins besides. He wanted nothing more than to commit every last one of those sins, with impunity, and with her. Cairo was only a man, after all, and he knew better than most what a terrible one he was, straight through to his core. And Brittany was sprawled across his lap, dressed in a sleek red corset and very little else, tasting of mint and longing.

He shifted, opening his mouth against hers, and he lost himself in the fire of it. The sheer, exultant perfection of the scrape of her tongue against his, the press of her breasts against his chest, the way she clung to his shirt as if she wanted him even a small fraction as much as he wanted her.

Cairo could work with a fraction.

He poured everything he had into the kiss, taking her mouth again and again. Lust and need. All the dark longings that had haunted him since she'd walked away from him in Monaco. All the sweet, hot desire that had flashed through him as he'd watched her performance here tonight.

All the fire in his twisted, haunted soul.

He wasn't surprised when she tore her mouth from his, and his arms tightened around her as if he expected her to twist out of his hold. She didn't—and it was a measure of how out of control he'd become that he counted that as a victory.

"I don't want anything to do with you," she hissed at him.

Cairo couldn't blame her. Neither did he. But that was beside the point.

"Of course not," he agreed, their lips practically touching, his hands full of her sweetness. "I can tell by the way you kiss me."

And then he set his mouth to hers once more.

Because kissing Brittany, he discovered quickly, was fast becoming his favorite vice in a life fairly overflowing with them.

This time when she pulled away, he discovered his hands had found their way to her thick hair in its tempting copper twist, and he'd pulled the fragrant curtain of it down around them. Her lips were sweet and full, her breath came as fast as his did, and her eyes had gone wide and dark.

Cairo thought he might never get enough of her, and it was a measure of how obsessed he was already that the notion failed to alarm him.

"You can't do this," she told him, and he had the strange thought that this was the real Brittany, after all her edge and flair. She sounded a little bit shaken. She looked a little bit fragile. He should have felt a surge of triumph at that, but instead, the thing that turned over inside him felt a good deal more like regret. He knew all about *regret.* "You know you can't."

"I don't think you've been paying attention, *cara,*" he told her, and he shifted one hand from her thick, gorgeous hair to drag his thumb over the plump seduction that was her lower lip. He ached to taste her again. He didn't know how he refrained. "I am the last of the Santa Dominis. Some still call me a king. I can do as I wish."

"Not with me, you can't." She jerked her mouth back from his touch and shoved her way to a more vertical sitting position on his lap, and the sweet agony of it all threatened to unman him where he sat. "I want nothing to do with your little game of lost thrones, thank you. My life is complicated enough."

"Marrying me would uncomplicate it."

"Right. Because that's exactly what you are. *Uncomplicated.*"

He could see the moment it occurred to her that despite

the hard tone she'd used, what she'd said might as well be a compliment. Little did she know. He could teach darkness to the night, and that was on his good days.

"I want to be inside you," he told her then, raw and untutored, as if he was a stranger to himself. He felt her shiver, as if the electric charge of it had seared straight through her. "So deep inside you, *cara*, that neither one of us can tell who is a king and who is a stripper. Until there is nothing in all the world but that sweet, wet heat and what burns us both as we drown in it."

He was close enough that he could see the way her pupils dilated at that, so close he could feel the goose bumps beneath his hand as easily as he could see them rise up all over her exposed skin. So close he could feel all that intense heat as it burned through her, like a wild flame incinerating them both.

"I can tell who is who, though," she said, and Cairo was certain he wasn't mistaking the sheer misery he could hear in her voice, as if this was as hard and mystifying a thing for her as it was for him. That was something. He told himself that had to be something. "Just as the tabloids certainly can. And I doubt that would ever change."

"Why would you wish it to change?" He hardly sounded like himself. Or maybe he'd forgotten what it was like to be so honest, about anything. His whole life was a collection of misdirection and straight-out lies, wrapped tight around the blackened, shriveled heart of a man who should have died years ago. "You've crafted your public persona with exquisite precision. Why not take it to its logical end?"

"I know exactly where my public persona is taking me," she gritted out at him. She shifted in his lap, brushing up against the part of him that yearned for her the most, and they both froze. She swallowed, her eyes dark on his, and he had the most absurd notion that she looked *panicked* for a moment. "And it's not to your bed."

"That is why you melt against me, I am sure. Why you cannot look away."

"I'm trapped in your lap. *You* are trapping me."

"We're in a public place," he continued, and though his palms itched to move over her, to learn her in the best and most tactile way possible and prove his point besides, Cairo didn't do it. He let his voice cast that spell instead. "How many people do you think are watching us instead of the stage?"

"All of them." He didn't imagine the sheen of something harder in her gaze then, or the way she tilted her chin up. "You saw to that."

"And yet, were I to slip my fingers just a little bit higher, what would I find?" He moved the hand on her thigh a scant centimeter higher, letting his fingers toy with the satin edge of her underwear. Her breath came in a rush even as she shivered out the truth again. "How wet are you, Brittany? Right here in a strip club where everyone can see you? Would you even protest if I slid my hand beneath those silly red underthings? Or would you lean in closer so no one could be sure and ride my hand instead?"

"Neither." But her voice was soft then. Too soft. As soft as he imagined she was only a fraction of an inch from the place his hand lingered. "I'm going to stand up and get back to work."

"Work?" Cairo laughed and moved his fingers again, and the flush on her delicate cheekbones told him she felt that precisely where he wanted her to feel it. So did he. "This place is an ill-mannered salute to your late husband's family, not your work. We both know what your true calling is."

Her lips pressed together and that melting heat in her dark hazel eyes faded. "If you mean that I'm a whore, you'll have to come up with a better insult. My mother's used the word so many times I've come to consider it an endearment."

"Then marry me," he heard himself say, quite as if it was a real proposal and he was truly as raw and ruined and *desperate* as he felt inside just then. As if there was any real thing inside him at all, when he knew better. But no matter that he told himself he was playing a role, he couldn't seem to stop this electric collision course he found himself on. Worse, he didn't want to stop it. "And we shall see what words your mother uses to address my queen."

"Evidence has never persuaded my mother away from the things she's decided are true," Brittany said, and what was remarkable, Cairo thought, was how she didn't sound bitter at all just then. Only matter-of-fact. It made that same temper he couldn't afford to indulge flare inside him all over again. "But thank you. I'm sure a season as queen to the King of Wishful Thinking would be a delight. But my dance card is full." She nodded at the stage before them. "Literally."

And this time, Cairo felt a kind of hitch in his chest when she pulled away from him. He let her stand, and watched her as she stood there before him, making no attempt to hide the evidence of his need. Her cheeks burned, her eyes gleamed dark, that marvelous copper hair of hers tumbled all around her in unruly waves, and Cairo understood that role or no, he would never, ever rest until he had her.

In his bed, to start.

But no other queen would do. He ignored the part of him that questioned that—the part that reminded him he was a king without a throne and in need of any unacceptable woman to make sure he stayed without it—and indulged the part of him that had the blood of five hundred years of Santa Dominis pounding in his blood. Five hundred years of autocratic rulers who knew what they wanted and took what they wished, and brooked precious little disagreement as they did it.

He might have lost his kingdom. He might never set foot in the palace his family had built from a primitive fortress into a splendid fairy tale ever again. But he was still who he was, who he'd been bred to be, and no matter the darkness he knew he carried inside of him—or else how could he make himself such a believable disgrace?—none of that mattered in the end. He was still Cairo Santa Domini.

"You can't have me," she told him, as if she could read his mind. As if she could see the truth of him, stamped in his bones, deep in his veins, all the kings and queens who'd gone before him.

"Silly girl," he drawled, and made no attempt to sit up straighter from his lazy position. Or to rein in the desire he was certain she could see stamped all over him, from his face to his sex. "Don't you know that only makes me want you more?"

"You'll have to learn to live with the disappointment somehow," she said dismissively, and Cairo only smiled.

"That," he murmured, like the threat it was, "is one thing you can depend upon me never, ever to do."

Brittany woke late the following morning in her little flat, four narrow flights up in a weathered old building on the outskirts of Montmartre. It was laughably tiny, although if she stood on a chair in her small kitchen there was enough of a view of the Parisian rooftops and the smallest bit of the famous Basilica of Sacré-Cœur that she could forget her worries a while as she craned her head to see a sliver of its pale white dome.

She did not think about what had happened the night before. She did not think about the dreams that had haunted her through the night, waking her again and again until she finally fell into something dreamless and exhausted near dawn.

She didn't think about any of it and yet she could still feel Cairo's touch. She could still taste him on her lips.

Her body was still in that insane tumult over him, from her breasts that felt swollen to twice their size, to the shivery hot knot low in her belly that clenched and clenched and clenched. Her body, which was supposed to be entirely hers. Her body, which she'd kept a pristine little fortress ever since her first wedding night, when she'd hidden from the whiny boyfriend turned drunken lout and had decided, there and then, that she'd rather die untouched and alone than let anyone else touch her against her will.

She'd never imagined that her body and her mind could disagree about what *her will* was.

Brittany took a very long shower to wash the night away. Then she went on her daily run at her gym, moving much faster than usual today through her usual miles, but the dreams and the memories stuck with her no matter how quick her pace.

It was never a good sign when the treadmill felt more like a metaphor than simple exercise.

Brittany was already in a dark, uneasy mood when she made it back to her flat. It did not improve when she picked up the private mobile phone she'd left plugged in on her bedside table to see her mother had called at least three times.

She was scowling at the screen as she scrolled through the logged calls, no messages, when it lit up with a fourth call from her mother.

Something cold snaked down Brittany's spine. The last time her mother had called repeatedly like this, Brittany's former stepchildren—all old enough to be her parents, a fact that perhaps only she and Jean Pierre had found amusing—had taken to the tabloids to sound the trumpets about how shoddily they'd treated her and how they had "expunged that harlot" from the family home at last.

Brittany's mother had not called to commiserate about yet another tour through the slag heaps of the tabloids. She'd called, as ever, to complain that her daughter's disgraceful behavior was humiliating the whole of the Hollis clan back in Gulfport and *had Brittany no shame?*

"Do you want me to have shame, Mom?" Brittany had asked coolly. Someday, she'd vowed for the nine millionth time, she would stop answering her mother's calls altogether. Someday when she'd finally come to terms with the fact that the woman was never, ever going to treat her as anything more than a source of income. Much less love her. *Someday.* "Or do you want me to keep paying your rent?"

Today was not *someday*, regrettably, but Brittany tossed the mobile aside without answering, letting her mother go to voice mail. She powered up her laptop instead.

She didn't even have to Google herself, as she sometimes did. Oh, no. The headlines were right there on her launch page.

His Royal Stripper?
How Low Can Cairo Go?
Black Widow Brittany Trades Up!

Her heart was already causing a commotion in her chest as she clicked on the first article, as if she already knew what she'd see—

But it was worse.

Someone had taken a series of pictures in the club last night. And the pictures made the whole thing look much more sordid than Brittany remembered it. Much hotter.

Much more desperate and *much* more public. If she hadn't known better, Brittany might have assumed that Cairo actually had bought her for the evening. The papers certainly insinuated he had.

He might as well have, she thought now. It came to the same thing, and if she'd let him, she'd have a paycheck to comfort herself this morning. Meanwhile, that scraped-raw, heavy feeling in her chest wasn't going to help a soul. It was better to ignore it. Starting with the little sound she didn't mean to let out as she sat there gaping at those awful pictures that told her far too many hard truths about herself and her own longings. She lifted up a hand to try to rub that harsh, hollow feeling out of her own chest.

It didn't really work.

She felt betrayed. By herself, not by the devastatingly handsome man whose entire life was a monument to wreck and ruin. She should have seen this coming. She should have known there was no way *Cairo Santa Domini* could turn up in her life *without* leaving his dark mark all over her.

This was what he did. Exactly this.

She should have assumed not only that someone would have photographed the whole of their encounter, but also that, of course, they'd sell it to the voracious tabloids. In point of fact, it was likely Cairo had engineered the whole thing and the photographer in question was on his payroll. Why hadn't she thought of that last night? *Of course* he'd play this up to the paparazzi. *This was what he did.*

She should have been prepared for this—why wasn't she?

But she knew why. Brittany hadn't been thinking after that kiss, which looked even more carnal and impossibly sexy in the pictures than she remembered it. And her memories were explicit. She hadn't been thinking when she'd staggered away from him and hid backstage, where none of the other girls talked to her and she could pretend she was utterly at peace as she changed back into her street clothes. She hadn't been thinking when she'd opted to walk home despite the hour and the questionable neighborhood, hoping the exercise and the night air might clear her head.

He'd kissed her. She'd kissed him. It had been the most sensual experience of her life, and she hated herself for that. She hated that she'd responded to him like that.

That kiss had been the only thought in her head.

The truth was, she hadn't been doing a whole lot of actual thinking since she'd walked into that casino in Monaco.

The fact that Cairo was certain to destroy her had loomed so large inside of her from her first glimpse of him that even now, it was making it hard for her to breathe. It was clouding her judgment, confusing her, making her *react* to him rather than act in her own best interests the way she always had before.

The way she'd been doing all her life, or she'd never have made it this far.

"Pull yourself together, Brittany," she ordered herself, her own voice loud in the quiet of her little studio, her own face much too big and exposed on the laptop screen before her, looking vulnerable and needy and entirely too aroused.

It horrified her to see that expression. Or it thrilled her, because she could still *feel* that kiss.

Or maybe she couldn't tell the difference. "This is an opportunity. Since when do you turn down an opportunity?"

Destruction wasn't a good enough excuse to avoid something. If it was, she'd never have left Gulfport at sixteen in the company of Darryl, whom she'd known perfectly well was nothing but trouble.

The kind of destruction Cairo was likely to cause, she understood in the wake of his kiss in a way she hadn't before, was purely internal. He wouldn't take a swing at her the way Darryl had. He might rip out her heart with his royal hands. He might tear it into pieces, mash it into a pulp beneath his feet. She didn't understand why a man she should find laughable in any real sense instead posed such a risk for her neglected little heart, but there it was. She didn't know why. She only knew it was an inescapable truth. She'd known it the moment she'd laid eyes on him.

"But so what?" she asked herself now, digging the heel of one palm into her chest as if that could make the feeling of immensity and inevitability go away.

Because other than the small issue of her inevitable ruin, Cairo Santa Domini was perfect for her purposes. More than perfect. He was *Cairo Santa Domini*—he was a dream come true. Richer than sin, possessed of more blue blood in the tip of one toe than her entire family tree put together and not in the least put off by her sad, tacky and deeply checkered past. Most of the wealthy European men Brittany had met after marrying Jean Pierre, including his own sons, had indicated that they would be happy to sully themselves with her in private of an afternoon, but would never allow anyone to see them in her gauche presence in public, lest their ancient claims to aristocracy collapse into so much deeply inferior dust.

Cairo was quite the opposite.

And if she still felt that strange pang at the fact he wanted her *because* of the image she'd crafted instead of despite it, to say nothing of her low-class upbringing, well…of course he did. Why else would a man like him notice a woman like her? That silly *pang* was between her and the heart he was going to break without even trying very hard, and the truth was, she could as easily live on her far-off island with a shattered heart as without it.

The point was the palm trees and the fruity drinks and the solitude. Who cared what happened to her heart?

So when her other mobile phone rang—the one she kept for paparazzi, tabloids and whoever else wanted to reach her yet didn't know her personally—she answered it.

"Please hold for His Serene Grace the Archduke Felipe Skander Cairo of Santa Domini," the cultured voice on the other end of the line intoned.

Brittany didn't hang up, despite that spike in her pulse. Because her own internal destruction was a small price to pay. Cairo Santa Domini might be as dangerous as he seemed. After last night, she knew he was.

But he was her only escape. He was the light at the end of the tunnel as much as he was also the train.

She had no choice.

"Darling," she purred when he came on the line, that voice of his dark and sinful and good enough to eat. God, she was in so much trouble. But she told herself it would all be worth it. One day, all of this would be worth it. Vanuatu waited for her across the planet, white sand beaches, peace and anonymity at last. "I saw our engagement announcement in all the tabloids. You shouldn't have."

CHAPTER FOUR

CAIRO APPEARED IN so many tabloids with so many women that even when the woman in question was notorious in her own right, like Brittany, it could only cause so much comment. There was the initial carrying on and then it was on to the next set of celebrity shenanigans. Football players were forever embroiling themselves in bitter custody disputes with B-list actresses, politicians were ever hypocritical and blustery in turn and the papers never lacked for seedy stories to tell in their breathless, insinuating headlines.

"We appear to be less interesting than the custody tussles of a striker for Real Madrid," Brittany said brightly when they met after the initial frenzy started to fade that first week, to plot out their next few moves. That sweet smile she could produce on cue did absolutely nothing to soften the edge in her voice—which was a good thing, Cairo thought, since he was a perverse creature who liked the edge better. "The entire world has been overexposed to Cairo Santa Domini scandals. A few pictures in a strip club are too run-of-the-mill to captivate the public interest after a steady diet of far worse. I'm afraid your shenanigans are good for a shudder, nothing more."

"It's usually more than a shudder," Cairo assured her, because he couldn't seem to help himself. "It's really more of a drawn-out scream, with many a religious conversion along the way. Oh, God. Oh, Cairo. *Oh, God.*"

Brittany sighed as if he was a deep and enduring trial to her. A sound Cairo was certain no woman—no *person*—had made in his presence in all his life, except himself.

"I'll keep that in mind," she said, as if placating a child having a tantrum.

"You do that," he murmured, and then they discussed how best to prepare for the second phase of their plan.

Cairo very rarely appeared with any woman more than once. It was difficult to maintain a reputation as an inveterate playboy if he seemed interested in quality rather than quantity, so he'd never tied himself down to anyone for more than a long weekend. Sometimes he'd throw in a repeated date or weekend years later, just to keep people guessing, but that didn't happen very often.

"I become rather boring after three consecutive days," he'd once told a smarmy journalist in Rome when questioned about this pattern of his, flashing a knowing smile as if he could already read the fan letters his secretary would be forced to wade through, each declaring him anything but *boring*. Some complete with enclosed panties, as punctuation. "It is less a pattern and more of a public service, you understand."

The second time the paparazzi "caught" him and Brittany in the sort of restaurant famous people would only patronize if they were trying to avoid being seen, five days after that night in the strip club, it caused a buzz. It suggested that an actual relationship of some kind had survived both what was called *Cairo's Scandalous Lap Dance* and the resultant tabloid screeching over the photos of the two of them kissing.

"Had I known this would cause such a commotion," Brittany told the pack of cameramen who surrounded her when she emerged from an expertly timed trip to Cartier, flashing her megawatt gold digger's smile and a sizeable cocktail ring on her right hand featuring a deep blue sapphire the approximate size of the Mediterranean Sea, "I would have asked for something a whole lot bigger."

Then, days after that dinner, they were seen exiting Cairo's private residence in the unfashionable morning light, suggesting they'd spent the night there. Or perhaps several days *and* nights, now that Brittany had finished her run at the strip club.

"Are you *dating*?" a clearly appalled television tabloid reporter asked Cairo as he made his way through the heaving mass of paparazzi outside a charity event in London a few days later. "You and the Queen of Tacky?"

"You will be the first to know." He smiled, all teeth and noblesse oblige. "You and all of your viewers are foremost in my thoughts as I navigate my romantic life, I assure you."

"Why isn't she with you tonight?" another reporter demanded. A bit too hotly, Cairo thought, as if these people had personal stakes in Cairo's continuing bachelorhood. He supposed they did. And in that darkness in him he paraded around in so many fine clothes, calling it a man and letting them call him the worthless one he'd always known he was. "Did you already break up?"

"I cannot keep track of this relationship according to all your conflicting headlines," he told them. "On, off. Playboy, gold digger. Maybe she and I are simply two people who enjoy each other's company. But of course, that makes no snide headlines for you, so that will never be printed as a possibility."

Cairo Calls Bad-news Britt a Gold Digger, screamed the papers the following day, right on cue.

After that, Cairo squired Brittany to the lavish wedding of an old boarding school friend of his, currently one of the richest men in Spain. The speculation about what they meant to each other surged into what could only be called a dull roar.

Had Cairo ever attended a wedding with a date before, therefore keeping him from finding several dates there? Answer: no. Did a man who was only after a bit of fun take that fun to a very old friend's wedding in the first place? Answer: of course not, as there was nothing fun about a date with high expectations that a man was only going to dash cruelly. The papers were agog. Could Cairo Santa Domini possibly be getting serious about the most unsuitable woman in the world—even after she'd finished her stint in that horrible Parisian club?

Answers on that last varied, especially after "a wedding guest" released a photo of Cairo and Brittany in their wedding finery, clinging to each other on the dance floor in what was called "the would-be king at his most tender and affectionate—friends claim they've never seen playboy Cairo lose his head like this before!"

"I had no idea you could dance so well with your clothes on," he'd murmured to her as they'd swayed to the wedding band.

"How many of the bridesmaids here have experienced what *you* do so well without your clothes?" she'd replied, not missing a step as she smiled up at him, and he was certain only he could see how razor-sharp that smile was.

After that, they took it to a new level and introduced a series of romantic holidays.

First a weekend in Dubai. Then a week in sun-drenched Rio, and an endless series of photographs of the happy couple on the famous beaches in very, very little. "The better," one online gossip magazine asserted dryly beneath a photo of Brittany in a tiny bikini, "to remind you why Brittany Hollis is dating your husband Cairo Santa Domini and you aren't." Then, after a low-key week or so in Paris, they embarked on an elaborate fortnight in Sub-Saharan Africa, from the sweeping deserts of Namibia to the glory of Victoria Falls to an elegant, fully catered safari in Botswana.

All photographed extensively and then carefully curated to look like a sweepingly luxurious trip so epic it redefined romance. A love letter to all the world, from two of the least likely people to fall in love around. A masterpiece.

If Cairo said so himself.

"Oh, please," Brittany replied when he actually did say it, sitting on one of the camp chairs in the spacious tent they shared, piled high with rugs and linens and tables laden with succulent foods, that had been set up for them a stone's throw from the nearby river bristling with hippos and crocodiles. She was reading yet another book on her e-reader while he tracked their headlines on his mobile, and they were the only ones in the entire world who knew that they slept on opposite sides of that tent the same way they'd slept in different parts of all the hotel suites he'd booked. Night after torturous night, not that it was driving him mad. "*Romance* is not the word being used when people discuss us. I think you know that."

He did know it. What he didn't know, out there in the deep Botswanan night so thick with stars, was why he wanted to change the conversation. Or why some part of him hated it every time another tabloid skewered her. When that, of course, had been the whole point from the start.

Has Brittany Stripped Her Way into Cairo's Heart? howled one New York gossip rag.

Will Cairo Be Lucky Number Four for Much-wed Brittany? asked a British paper, pretending to be slightly less salacious.

Another British paper was far less circumspect: *Brittany's Big-game Hunt in Botswana—Will She Nab Herself a Crown?*

And more starkly by far, in the most popular Santa Domini paper over a picture of the two of them gazing adoringly at each other: *Queen Brittany?*

He should have been pleased, Cairo told himself. Everything was going according to plan. He should have been *exultant*.

But he didn't sleep much on that holiday, and he told himself it had nothing to do with the fact she was in that tent with him, yet a world away. He told himself it was for the best, and he should *exult* in the fact this woman seemed so immune to him.

Exult, he told himself as they smiled and laughed and pretended so well the whole world gasped and carried on over every new photograph.

Exult, he ordered himself when they were in private and she held herself so far away, all cool smiles and distance and her face forever in a book.

He shouldn't find her a mystery and he shouldn't want so badly to solve that mystery that he was up half the night. If this was exulting, Cairo thought as the safari wrapped up and they returned to their regularly scheduled lives in Europe, he was going to require a whole lot more caffeine to survive all the nights he spent asking himself if she really was the only woman he'd ever met who saw only the darkness in him.

That and why, if she was, he was masochistic enough to find that attractive.

"I'm getting the sense that the world is not so much rejoicing in our relationship or even avidly watching it unfold so much as they're craning their necks at us, the way people do at a terrible accident," Brittany said as they flew back to Paris from an exceptionally glorious charity ball in Vienna one night.

She set aside the paper she'd been reading and eyed Cairo as he lounged on the sofa across from her in his preferred position: lying flat on the white leather sectional with his feet propped up on the far arm, his dark suit in disheveled disarray all around him because the more rumpled he looked, the more the papers speculated about his sexual prowess and giddily imagined he performed sex acts behind every potted plant in Europe.

Who was he to deny his public?

He waved a negligent hand and let the ice cubes rattle around in the drink he held. The more noise the ice cubes made, he'd discovered long ago, the drunker people assumed he was. And it was astonishing, the things people said and did when they assumed another person was too drunk to remember, respond or protest.

Cairo wondered if he'd ever simply live through a moment, without mounting any kind of performance to survive it. Or if he even knew how to do that, when there was nothing in him but lies atop lies.

Then he wondered why, when it had been this way since he was a young man, he found the realities of his life and all its necessary untruths so terribly constricting now.

"We are a delicious accident, *cara*," he told her, and experimented with a faint, fake slurring of his words. "That's the whole point."

"My mistake," Brittany replied. "I was starting to think the point was you cavorting about the globe so you could better rub your wealth and careless lifestyle in the face of every last person alive."

"That is a mere side benefit. One I greatly enjoy."

Cairo swung around to sit up, raking his hair back from his forehead as he did. He put his drink down on the coffee table in the expansive jet cabin that better resembled a hotel suite, and he told himself there was no reason in the world for this *gnawing* thing inside him.

She'd agreed to everything after that night in the strip club. After that kiss he'd been torturing himself with ever since, as if it had been his first. She'd come to his residence in the car he'd sent for her in the middle of the night that week, to keep the meeting a secret. All the hints he'd seen of some kind of vulnerability in the strip club had been gone by then. Long gone, leaving her as smooth as glass. She'd merely discussed their strategy with him, offered her own thoughts and ideas and then signed all the papers. No theatrics. No hint of any emotion at all, as if everything between them was strictly business.

Brittany had insisted that was how it should remain.

"You must be joking," Cairo had protested after she'd dropped that little bomb. It had been well into the wee hours that night in Paris, and she'd sat there across from him in one of his ecstatically baroque salons as if she'd been carved from stone.

"I rarely joke at all," she'd replied, deadpan. "And never about sex."

"But sex is one of the great joys of life. Surely you must know this."

"No wonder you are widely held to be such a bright beacon of happiness. Oh, wait. Laziness is more your style, isn't it, Your Indolent Majesty?"

He hadn't known quite what to make of such a strange, stilted conversation about sex with a woman whose taste was still tearing him apart. A woman who, even then, had that same high color on her cheeks that told him she wanted him as badly as he wanted her, no matter what cold, repressive things she said to deny it.

"I know you want me," Cairo had said, baldly. As if he'd never finessed a situation in his life. As if he didn't know how. As if he couldn't help himself or keep himself from being more alarmingly honest with this woman than he was with anyone else alive. "Do you imagine you're hiding it?"

"I don't care who you sleep with, of course," Brittany

had continued as if he hadn't said a word. She'd waved a negligent hand in the air, but he'd seen the way her eyes glittered. He'd been certain that meant something. Or he'd wanted, desperately, for that to mean something. "I only ask that you keep it discreet, so as not to distract from what we're trying to accomplish, and that you make certain to keep it far away from me. That's only courteous."

"No threesomes, then?" he'd asked. Drawled, really. Entirely to watch her reaction—but she'd given him nothing but that glass exterior of hers, smooth and clear.

"You can have all the threesomes you like." Her brows had arched and he'd felt skewered on that hard gaze of hers. "Unless, of course, a man of your appetites finds that number restrictive. Believe me when I tell you I couldn't care less where you put your, ah, royal scepter. As long as it isn't anywhere near me."

"That's hurtful." He cocked his head to one side as he considered her. "My scepter is considered the toast of Europe, if not the entire world."

A faint gleam in her dark eyes then. "I doubt that."

"Naturally, the savage, rutting creature you seem to think I am will only view your denial of what we both feel as a great challenge."

"I don't feel anything." Her voice then had been crisp, her gaze clear, but he still hadn't believed her. Wishful thinking or the truth? How could he still not know? "Am I attracted to you? Of course. You're a remarkably handsome man. I can't imagine any woman alive wouldn't react to you, especially when you decide to turn all of that smoldering on her to get your way."

"Is that what I did? I thought I kissed you and you kissed me back and we very nearly broke a few decency laws right there in that strip club. It wouldn't have bothered me if we had. I have an unofficial diplomatic immunity. You, of course, might not enjoy a stint in a French prison."

"I don't find it necessary to act on every attraction I might feel," Brittany had said, again as if he hadn't spoken. He hadn't been able to think of any other person alive who'd ever treated him as if he was annoying. What was the matter with him that he found that as intriguing as anything else she did? How much must he hate himself? But, of course, he'd already known the answer to that. And she'd still been speaking, still fixing him with that stern glare of hers that he'd doubted she knew made him almost painfully hard. "And I feel certain that as time goes on, the attraction will fade anyway."

"I'm told that never happens. Such is my charm." Cairo had smiled when she'd shaken her head at that. "I'm only reporting what others have said."

"How would they know?" she'd retorted, settling back in her chair as if its stuffy, hard back was comfortable so long after 2:00 a.m. "You never spend more than a weekend with anyone. I'm signing up for far more exposure to your…"

"My scepter?" he supplied.

Her smile in return had been that sharp, edgy thing he found far too fascinating. "Your charm. Such as it is."

"I think you're kidding yourself," he'd said softly then, because he couldn't seem to maintain his game with this woman. "Sex is inevitable."

"I'm sure you believe that," she'd replied, her tone crisp, as if she didn't care either way, and he'd found that needled him far more than if she'd seemed horrified. "And I told you I don't care who you have it with, so I certainly don't need to hear about it." Then she'd shrugged as if she'd never encountered a topic more tedious in all her life. "Have at, with my blessing."

Except the most curious thing had happened since that conversation. Cairo had discovered that he hadn't had the slightest urge to touch any woman but her. He told himself it was because she'd proven herself to be such an excellent partner. A perfect costar in this little bit of theater they were performing for the masses and for their own complementary ends.

He told himself a lot of things. But the only woman he saw was her.

"Why would you do this?" she'd asked him that first night when Ricardo had ushered her into the elegant salon that had stood more or less unchanged for centuries. "What can you possibly hope to gain?"

He'd only shrugged. "I need an infliction, as you said, for any number of shallow reasons. Why are you doing it?"

She'd sniffed. "I want to retire to Vanuatu and live on the beach, where no one can take a single photograph of me, ever."

Cairo didn't think they'd believed each other, but there it was. And here they were now, weeks into this thing. She dressed perfectly, reacted perfectly, gazed at him with the perfect mix of adoration and mystery whenever there was a camera near. She was tailor-made for her role.

That had to be why he'd lost his drive for his favorite vices, women and whiskey, in no particular order. He was too busy taking in the show.

"Why are you staring at me like that?" she asked now.

She'd changed from her stunning ball gown the moment they'd boarded the plane, almost as if she couldn't bear to be in all that couture a moment longer. She did it every time. The moment she could be certain no cameras would follow her, she threw off all the trappings of her larger-than-life presence and left nothing behind but a real, live woman.

Cairo was fascinated. He found he liked her in what he considered her backstage uniform. Low-slung, high-end athletic pants that clung to every lithe curve and long-sleeved T-shirts made of the light, remarkably soft cotton she preferred. Usually, like tonight, she also wore an oversized cashmere scarf she would wrap several times around her neck. He liked it. He liked her gleaming copper hair piled high on the top of her head, so he could see her delicate ears and the line of her neck and that sweet, soft nape he had every intention of getting his mouth on, one of these days.

"Forgive me," he said when moments dragged by and he was still staring. "It occurred to me that you're the only woman I've ever seen in casual clothes." He smiled, and had no idea why it seemed to come less easily than usual. "My lifestyle has never really leant itself to such intimacies."

Brittany blinked. Then again. Her expression shifted from that bulletproof cool he despised and admired in turn to something else. Something that made that gnawing thing in him dig deeper and start to actually hurt.

"You work so hard to pretend otherwise," she said after a moment that dragged on far too long and made his chest hurt. "But beneath all the smoke and mirrors, beneath the Cairo Santa Domini spectacle, you're a completely different man. Aren't you?"

Cairo didn't like that at all. He'd worked too hard for too long to make certain no one ever bothered to take him at anything but face value, because he knew exactly how black and cold it was beneath. Why was this woman the only person on earth who never seemed to do that?

"There is no 'beneath the spectacle.'" His voice was too grim. Too gritty. Too damned revealing. "There is only spectacle. The spectacle is how I survive, Brittany. Believe that, if nothing else."

It was possibly the most honest thing he'd ever said to her. Or to anyone.

"Sometimes I think you're a monster," she told him. "I think you want me to think it. And then other times…"

Her voice softened, and everything inside him ran hot and wild, terror and need. "I think you're possibly the loneliest man I've ever met."

His heart kicked at him. Cairo wanted to kick back. At her, and this situation, at his whole wasted, twisted life.

"I don't know an orphan or refugee who is ever anything else," he said quietly. He knew he shouldn't have said it. He should have made a joke, laughed it off. Said something appalling or shallow, as expected. But he couldn't seem to look away from her. He couldn't seem to breathe. He didn't understand what was happening to him or why he couldn't stop it. There was nothing in all the world but her lovely face and that searing gleam of recognition in her dark hazel eyes, and the words coming out of his mouth, filled with a truth he knew he shouldn't tell. "I am both. All I have—all I will ever have—is the spectacle."

He slumped back down after that, pretending to lapse off instantly into sleep like the lazy ass he was so good at playing would.

But he felt the weight of her dark gaze on him for a long time after.

"The general is rumored to be in ill health," Ricardo told him some days later. "It has been widely suggested that this ill-conceived fling of yours at a time the kingdom might actually need you may finally have put you beyond the pale, even in the eyes of your most die-hard supporters."

Cairo did not look up from his laptop, where he was managing his investment portfolio with a shrewdness he knew most would not believe he possessed, but then, he had worked hard to live down to any and all expectations. He sat at the gleaming, polished table in his Parisian residence that had welcomed all manner of European royalty in its time. It, like everything else in this house he'd inherited from his late family and got to rule over like the high king of ghosts, was a monument to nostalgia.

He included himself in that tally.

"I would have thought that I was so many shades lighter than pale that I'd gone entirely translucent before my eighteenth birthday," he said, more to the screen than to Ricardo. "That was certainly the goal." He sat back then and eyed the closest thing he had in the world to a friend, this man who had been at his side since before his family had died and who would support him to the bitter end. "What will it take? A murder conviction?"

"The loyalists would only claim you'd been framed, Sire. And then you'd simply be in prison, a situation that I doubt would suit you."

Cairo did not state the obvious: that he was already in prison. That he had been born into one sort of prison and then, after the revolution that had sent his family into exile, thrust into an entirely different one. And that the way he'd lived since he'd survived his adolescence was yet another jail cell, all things considered, no matter how elegantly appointed.

No one had any sympathy for a man like Cairo Santa Domini. Cairo, least of all. He knew he deserved it.

"You are correct," he said instead. "A life sentence would not suit me at all."

Ricardo smiled slightly, as if he knew exactly what Cairo hadn't said. "The scandal sheets are having a field day and there appear to be more than the usual number of appalled citizens registering their dismay at your antics, but I'm afraid the rumblings from the most deluded of your followers grow ever louder. It's as if they think they must act before you commit an unthinkable crime."

"Not an actual murder, I assume. A marriage." Ricardo nodded and Cairo rubbed a hand over his face. "But the general is unwell?"

His murderous heart, one of the many reasons he would never be a good man, wanted that evil man dead, as painfully as possible. It would be a good start.

"The palace is trying to keep it quiet, but my sources tell me it is serious," Ricardo said quietly. He aimed a swift, dark look from Cairo. "The loyalists think this relationship of yours is a distraction. Merely a game you play as you bide your time and wait for the usurper to die."

Cairo thought of the loyalists, true believers who had opposed the general's coup thirty years ago and had only grown stronger and louder in the years since. The more the general hunted them down and attempted to silence them, the louder they got and the more furiously they agitated for Cairo to return and take his throne.

They didn't seem to realize that his attempting to do so would lead to nothing but slaughter. Had they learned nothing from his family's "accident"? General Estes was as much a butcher today as he had ever been. Perhaps even more so, if his power was slipping away.

"The loyalists believe what they want to believe," he said now.

"The key points they wished me to pass on all concern your current companion," Ricardo told him. "She is inappropriate, they claim. Unacceptable, though stronger language was used. She is a slap, and I quote, 'in the face of centuries of the Santa Domini bloodline.'"

"Heaven forfend the bloodline that ends in me suffer a slap. The monarchy might be lost in shame forever—ah, but then, there is no monarchy and hasn't been for thirty years."

Ricardo had heard all of this before. He inclined his head. "They want to meet."

They did not want to do anything so innocuous as *meet*. They wanted to plan, to scheme. They wanted to talk strategies and possibilities. The practical loyalists wanted their seized lands and confiscated fortunes back. The idealists wanted the country of their forefathers, the fairy-tale perfection of "the kingdom in the clouds," as Santa Domini had been known in previous centuries. Cairo was as much a figurehead to them as he was to their enemies.

And figureheads too often ended up sacrificed to the cause, one way or another. What the loyalists failed to realize was that they'd be served up along with him. Cairo had been trying to avoid that very outcome since the general had assassinated his family.

As long as the general lived, nothing and no one Cairo cared about was safe.

"Impossible," he murmured now. "My social calendar is filled to bursting and I am, quite publically, falling head over heels in love with an American temptress reviled on at least three continents, rendering me stupendously unfit to be anyone's king."

"That is what I told them, more or less. It was not received well."

This was the problem with royal blood. History was littered with the executed and deposed relatives of this or that monarch, all of whom had been pressed into service by exactly the sort of people Cairo knew better than to actually speak to directly. The fact of his existence was enough of an irritant to General Estes. The general had claimed the throne of Santa Domini, but everyone knew he'd taken that throne by force and, because of that, there would always be whispers that he could only hold the throne by the same force. Meanwhile, Cairo hadn't set foot on Santa Dominian soil since he'd been a child and had made himself one part a laughingstock and two parts too scandalous to bear, but there was no doubt that he was his country's legitimate heir.

If he'd hid himself away somewhere and stayed out of the public eye as his parents had advised him to do when he was a child, Cairo wouldn't have survived to adulthood. That he lived, that he drew breath daily, was a constant reminder to the general that he was not legitimate and could never be legitimate no matter whom he bullied. That he had not won his position by popular vote or historic right, but by violence and betrayal.

Cairo had spent a very long time making sure no one could possibly imagine a known fool like him, vapid and excessive and usually scandalously naked besides, as any kind of king. Secret meetings and murky discussions with those who would use him to take back the country would undo all of that work. It would put not just Cairo at risk, but all of those who had ever supported his family. From the sweet nannies who had raised him and his lost sister, to Ricardo, to say nothing of the ancient families that had stood with the kings of Santa Domini for centuries.

He might have risked himself, now that he was no longer a grieving and terrified boy. But he had already lost everyone he'd ever cared about. He could not risk anyone else.

He would not.

"I suppose there is only one course of action, then," he said after a moment, when the air in the old room, so much like a mausoleum, grew tight. "To put the final nail in my coffin."

"Not literally, I hope." Because Ricardo would always do what was asked of him, Cairo knew this as well as he knew his own heart within his chest, but that didn't make the man any less of a loyalist at heart.

He made himself smile, and pretended, as he always did, that he didn't know how deeply the other man longed for Cairo to stand up one day and announce he'd had enough—that he was taking back the kingdom. That day would never come. Cairo had made certain of that, as surely as he'd made sure to become exactly the sort of creature his beloved father would have loathed.

"Indeed, that is what we always hope, Ricardo," he said instead, and for the first time in a long while, he found he actually meant it.

Cairo turned his attention back to his laptop, telling himself that he was perfectly calm, because he should have been. That his heart was not beating too hard, that he was not tense with sheer anticipation—for all the wrong things—because he should have been as composed as he was when he handled his investment portfolio.

That he was not should have concerned him a great deal more than it did.

Because it was finally time to propose to Brittany, his inappropriate consort who functioned as the perfect sucker punch against his splendid ancestry, royal blood and claim to the throne of Santa Domini.

He would make her his wife and ruin the dreams of all those loyal to him, once and for all.

He should have viewed this necessary step with a measure of satisfaction. Possibly with a touch of nostalgia for the country he'd not laid eyes on since he was small boy.

But he found that instead of his kingdom, what he thought about was Brittany. Copper fire and the sweet, hot insanity of her slick mouth against his. Her lean, muscled curves in his lap and her scent all around him like a fist. The torture of these last weeks, of having her so close and yet so far away. Every touch he stole in front of the cameras that he relived for another sleepless hour when alone at night. The agony of her smile, of that mysterious distance in her eyes. It had been unbearable from the start.

But the time had come at last.

He would finally, finally make her his.

Cairo found he couldn't wait.

CHAPTER FIVE

"PAY ATTENTION, PLEASE," Cairo said from across the small table, which was how Brittany realized she'd been lost in her own head somewhere. She snapped her gaze back to his and saw that same brooding, amused impatience in those caramel depths that she was starting to crave a little bit too much.

Maybe more than a little bit.

She shoved that thought aside and cranked up her smile to something melting and adoring, as befit the occasion. She assured herself it was completely feigned. She'd worn a gown of glorious red that clutched at her breasts and then tumbled down to flirt with her knees, and the sort of fancifully high and delicate shoes that impressed even the most glamorous French women. She'd pulled back the front part of her hair and let the rest of the heavy mass of it swirl down from that gleaming little clip to tumble past her bare shoulders, a sleek fall of copper that she knew caught the light.

She would look beautiful in all the engagement pictures. Elegant, even; the better for all the nasty "compare and contrast" photos the papers would run the moment they heard the news. This side a future almost-queen dressed for the part, that side a stripper in a G-string and a bikini top upside down on a pole.

The vicious articles wrote themselves.

Brittany told herself, the way she seemed to do more

and more these days, that she didn't mind at all. That this was what she wanted. That she was as pleased with the public persona she'd created as she ever had been, and welcomed the way she and Cairo were using it to their own ends.

I have never been happier in all my life, she told herself now, surrounded by fine china and Michelin stars. Again and again, hoping it would sink in. *Not ever.*

Cairo looked devastatingly gorgeous. Cairo always looked devastatingly gorgeous. The things the man did to a jacket and a pair of dark trousers defied description. It was as if a light shone upon him from a great height, making him seem something like angelic despite his rather more earthy reputation. He turned heads. He inspired sighs. He couldn't walk across an empty street without someone gasping aloud, and there'd been a chorus of dreamy sighs all the way across the restaurant floor when they'd entered.

He was the most dangerous man Brittany had ever met, and sometimes, when he lost that smirk of his and stopped saying his usual absurd and provocative things, she was sure it was as obvious to the world as it felt sloshing about inside her.

Tonight he'd chosen the best table in Paris's current darling of a restaurant, where the paparazzi could crowd about outside and take telephoto pictures of their meal. He'd picked her up from her flat in a flashy sports car, a muscular Italian bit of fancy in a deep, glossy black, and had swept her into the restaurant in a hail of flashbulbs that hardly seemed to register to him at all. A surreptitious glance at the mobile phone in her evening clutch told her the pictures were online before they'd ordered their first course.

There's no getting out of this, a little voice kept whispering to her from that place, deep inside her, where everything was fluttery and terrified and all because it recognized how susceptible she was to this man. How vulnerable. He made her *feel things* and that was unforgivable. *There's no taking it back.*

"You seem bored," Cairo said after one silent moment bled into the next. He leaned back in his chair in that exultantly male way of his, a negligent finger tracing the stem of his wineglass as he spoke. "Surely not."

From a distance she would look enthralled with him, she knew. Or she hoped. She leaned forward and rested her chin on her hand, to underscore that impression. Too bad it made it far too easy to forget that she was supposed to be acting.

"It's only that I've done this so many times before," she said.

Laughter flashed over his extraordinary face, and that didn't help. Brittany might as well have plugged herself into an electrical outlet and switched on the power to full blast. She *felt* it when he laughed. Everywhere.

She was in so much trouble. That truth shivered through her, making her stomach flip over and then knot tightly, and it took everything she had to pretend it wasn't actually happening.

Cairo watched her, close and hot, as if he knew every last thing she wanted to hide from him. "Did your teenage first husband propose to you in the finest restaurant in…wherever you came from?"

"In fact he did," she said loftily. Brittany forgot herself again and grinned at him, remembering. "It was the parking lot of a McDonald's with a bag of cheeseburgers from the drive-thru."

"Be still my heart."

"That counted as highly romantic to a sixteen-year-old girl with no prospects, I'll have you know. Darryl had even bought the cheeseburgers, which made the whole thing especially fancy."

He smiled at that. Brittany looked away. The sapphire ring she wore on her right hand caught the candlelight and reminded her exactly how far she'd come from a fast-food parking lot in Gulfport, Mississippi.

Cairo wasn't done. "And what about poor Carlos, who you treated so hideously on television like the callous creature the papers tell us daily you truly are?"

"He came into the bar where I was working—"

"Is that a euphemism? Do you mean another strip club?"

"I mean the bar where I was working as a waitress," she said, shaking her head at him. Then she relented. "The strip club was my second job."

Cairo's mouth moved into that smile of his that she'd discovered made her silly straight through. Completely and utterly foolish, and something like shattered besides. The only defense she had against it was to act like an icicle. But somehow, she couldn't seem to do that tonight. Her ability to freeze had disappeared, lost somewhere in the dancing flames of the candles between them. Or in that smile of his that made her feel like just another flickering bit of the light surrounding him.

Maybe it wasn't the worst thing, to be caught up in this man. To flicker and dance around him like the candles on the tables, or his loyal subjects, who followed him from party to party without end, or every woman who'd ever laid eyes on him. Maybe she was trying too hard to resist the inevitable. It was possible that giving in to it would make this latest transactional, cold-blooded marriage… easier.

Sweeter, anyway. She had to believe it would make it so much sweeter.

"Carlos came into the bar and he said he was moving

to Los Angeles and I should go with him." She shrugged away the other parts of the story that had little to do with what he'd asked. She didn't like to think about that time. The usually angry, rough clientele and the places they tried to put their hands. That ever-present sense of danger that, still, had been better than a life dodging Darryl's fists. She might have been a virgin, but her experiences had made sure she never felt anything like innocent. "He was pretty sure he could get us both on a television show if I did."

"Better than a sonnet."

"I asked what the catch was, because who walks around claiming they can get on television shows? He said we had to get married, I said okay. The end."

Cairo didn't actually move to put a hand over his heart, but the gesture was implied in the way he watched her then, his caramel gaze looking darker in the candlelight. More like whiskey than candy, and it made Brittany feel a little tipsy, instantly.

Maybe more than just a little tipsy, she thought.

"Sheer poetry," he said, his mouth in that tempting curve. "And Jean Pierre? Or did he have one of his nurses do the honors as he lay in his sickbed?"

"That one was much more fun." Brittany couldn't seem to stop smiling at him tonight, when she knew better. These past weeks had been sheer torture. Cairo was not the sort of man whose potency wore off the longer she spent time with him, like every other man she'd ever known. Not Cairo. He intensified. He got *worse.* "He came backstage after one of my shows."

"This time we really are talking about a strip club again, yes? For the purposes of clarity?"

"He said some lovely, complimentary things." She raised her brows at him, daring him to comment.

"I'm sure he praised the strip club's choreographer to the moon and back." Cairo nodded, that sharp gleam in his gaze telling her he knew very well Jean Pierre had done no such thing. "Or perhaps the set design?"

"Something like that," Brittany murmured.

Jean Pierre had told her something that bordered on filthy, that he'd somehow made sound charmingly bawdy instead—but Brittany suspected that Cairo, with that sharp gleam still in his gaze as he waited, wouldn't find it nearly as amusing as she had at the time.

She didn't want to dig into how she knew that. Much less what it meant.

"And then he told me he had very little time left to live and a handful of deeply ungrateful children. 'Marry me, *cherie*,' he said." She affected a dramatic French accent and had the enormous, very complicated pleasure of seeing Cairo's dark amber gaze gleam with pleasure. "'And we'll give them hell.'"

"This proved sufficiently compelling for you? I'll make a note."

"Jean Pierre had a certain charm."

"By which, of course, you mean his net worth."

There was no particular reason for that to slice through her, especially not tonight. Brittany didn't know what was the matter with her, especially because it was true. She didn't know why she felt so…fragile. She couldn't scowl at him with so many people watching them, inside the restaurant and out, so she had to settle for a bright sort of smile that made her own mouth hurt.

"I make no apologies for that or any other choice I made, then or now," she told him, and she chose not to concentrate on how difficult it was to keep her voice in the neighborhood of calm. "Only people who never have to worry about money look down on those who do nothing but. Besides—" she let her gaze sweep over him, from that reckless dark hair to his careless smile, and the sheer masculine beauty of that body of his he packaged to perfection "—you're no different from me."

"I must beg to differ, *cara.* I do not sell myself to the highest bidder."

Her smile still hurt. Worse, then. "Keep telling yourself that. Tabloid after tabloid after tabloid."

Cairo's eyes flashed with an emotion she couldn't read. He inclined his head slightly, very slightly. He did not say touché. Brittany supposed he didn't have to say it out loud. The fact she'd scored a direct hit seemed to simmer in the air between them.

"Cairo," she said, and she didn't know what she was doing. She was performing, yes, but all she wanted was to...do something about the fact it seemed she'd hurt him, when she'd have said that was impossible. "You're not the man you play in public." She didn't know where that came from, only that the moment she said it, something shifted inside her. She knew it was true. She reached her hand out across the table, but he didn't take it. "It won't kill you to admit that, if only to me."

He let a bitter sort of laugh, and Brittany had the impression he was as surprised by the sound as she was. He leaned forward. He still didn't reach for her hand.

"That is where you are wrong," he told her, and she went still. His dark eyes were so dark and something like tortured, and she realized in the same instant that she'd never seen him look like this. Not remotely indolent. Not the least bit lazy or pampered. No trace of that smirk on his beautiful mouth. "It very well might kill me. Did you imagine this was a game?"

That sat there between them, stark and harsh. Brittany's head spun. Then he pulled his gaze away and ran an unnecessary hand down the perfect line of his lapel.

"What do you mean by that?" she asked, her voice

barely above a whisper, her hand still reaching across the table. She couldn't seem to move a muscle.

"I mean nothing by it." But it took him another long moment to look at her again, and she didn't believe him. "I am a creature of well-documented extremes, that is all. The theater of it all goes to my head sometimes and I imagine I am starring in some great tragedy. I think we both know I am not the tragedy sort."

"Cairo…"

But he changed again, right there before her eyes. He didn't appear to move a muscle, and yet he changed. He looked as useless and lazy as ever, that stark moment gone as if it had never been.

"This proposal will be unmemorable, I'm sure," he told her, his voice amused and his gaze more like his usual caramel again. Light. Easy. Why couldn't she believe it? "Especially for a woman as vastly experienced in this area as you. Are you ready?"

Brittany pulled her hand back from the center of the table and told herself this was none of her business. *He* was none of her business. She should never have acted as if she wanted to know *the real him* anyway. What an exiled king chose to hide behind his public mask was his affair, not hers.

"It can't possibly be as heartwarming as cheeseburgers in a parking lot, or off-color remarks in a strip club," she replied, and it was a fight to make her voice cool again. As if that strange moment that still spiked the air between them hadn't happened. "But you do like a challenge, don't you?"

Cairo's mouth moved into its usual amused curve, though his eyes remained dark on hers. He reached into the pocket of his suit coat and pulled out a small box. An instantly identifiable jeweler's box that could really only contain one thing. And still, Brittany found herself staring at it as if she didn't know what it was. As if she didn't know what was happening. As if they hadn't decided he would do this here, now, tonight.

The frightening part was, she was only partially acting. She felt too hot, then too cold. Her tongue felt glued to the roof of her mouth.

He moved then, shifting from his seat to kneel down beside her chair, and her heart started drumming wildly in her chest. She couldn't tell if the restaurant around them went quiet. She couldn't tell if the earth had stopped spinning. The point of this was the spectacle he'd mentioned, the endless show that was both their lives—but all she could see was this. Him.

The last man in the world who should ever have been kneeling down before her, and yet there he was, doing exactly that.

The whole world narrowed as he took her hand in his.

Then disappeared entirely.

This isn't real, this isn't real, this isn't real, she chanted at herself.

But the truth was, it felt more than real. It felt like a fairy tale, the kind she'd lectured herself against loving or believing in all her life. It felt like magic and hope and something sweet besides.

His Serene Grace the Archduke Felipe Skander Cairo of Santa Domini smiled at her, Brittany Hollis, from the worst trailer park in Gulfport, Mississippi, as if she thrilled him. As if she really, truly did. That treacherous part of her, not buried as deep inside her as it should have been, wished that was possible. Oh, how she wished it.

He cracked open the small box he held and presented it to her with flourish, and Brittany's heart stopped.

She knew that ring. Everybody knew that ring. That glorious, incomparable diamond for which songs had been written and blood had been shed, across the ages. She knew its sparkle, its shape, even the delicate, precious stones that surrounded it like a whimsical halo. It had been painted by any number of great masters over the centuries, was known as one of the finest legacy jewels in all of Europe, and was so beloved by so many that various paste representations were sold all over the world.

"It was my mother's," Cairo said quietly, his eyes on hers. She knew that. He must have known that everybody alive knew that. "And my grandmother's before her, going back hundreds upon hundreds of years. It was commissioned a very long time ago, crafted by my kingdom's finest artisans, and is known as the Heart of Santa Domini. I hope you will wear it proudly."

"Cairo…" Her voice was a whisper. She couldn't wear such a ring. She couldn't bear it. It was a symbol of hope, of love, and this was nothing but a sideshow performance for a baying crowd. But she couldn't seem to open her mouth and tell him so.

She'd forgotten her internal chant entirely. She'd forgotten her own name. She'd forgotten the fact they were in public, the paparazzi right there outside the window, even the fact that all of this was staged.

There was only the look in Cairo's caramel gaze. That hot, dark, gleaming thing that wrapped around her and pulled tight. There was only the way he took that fairy-tale ring from the velvet box and then slid it onto her finger, as if she was the princess in the tale, not the joke he was playing on the world.

"Marry me," he said, and his voice was different, too. Deeper. Richer.

As raw as she felt.

And Brittany understood how foolish this game of theirs was. There was nothing the slightest bit cool about her then. No icicle. Nothing even close. She felt… everything. She didn't know if she wanted to cry or if she wanted to scream. If she wanted to fall into his arms or run away. She only knew that she'd been married three times and not one of them had ever felt like this. Not one of them had ever made her shake, inside and out.

Not one of them had ever been anything but expedient.

She tried to remind herself that Cairo was the same, if on a grander scale. That it was all he was. She tried to tell herself this was no different from the rest, and no matter that she was wearing one of the most romantic diamonds in the history of the world on her hand.

"Must I beg?" he asked then, though he looked as comfortable on one knee as he did lounging in a chair or sprawled out on a sofa. As if he could inhabit whatever posture he found himself in and make it his own, and easily.

"Of course not," she said quickly, and she wasn't faking the way she shook. Or the sting of tears that threatened to spill over from behind her eyes. "Of course you don't have to beg."

"Say it," he ordered her, every inch of him the king he wasn't, even as he kneeled in what ought to have been a supplicant position. It took her breath away. It made her imagine that all of this was something much, much different than it was, and that, she knew on some distant level, was the most dangerous thing of all. "I find I require it."

"Yes," she told him, this exiled king on his knees before her. *Her.* Brittany Hollis, reality-show villain and scourge of Europe, destined for nothing but infamy and then irrelevance. In that order, if she was lucky. "Yes, I'll marry you."

"I hoped you might." He didn't move. His eyes were lit up with that drugging heat she didn't want to recognize, but she did. God help her, but she did. She could feel it echo inside of her, making that sweet, hot knot in her belly bloom into something more like an ache. “Come now, Brittany. We need to sell this scene for our adoring public.”

“I said yes. What more do you want? A song and dance?”

“I think you know.” He smiled when all she did was stare at him, so outside herself she hardly knew where she was, and shivering inside as if she’d never get warm again. She wasn’t sure she wanted to. “Kiss me, please. And make it good.”

Brittany felt dizzy then. Hot and wild and pierced straight through.

But it didn’t occur to her not to obey him.

You want *to obey him*, that voice inside her accused her.

She sat forward in her seat. She let go of his hand and indulged that part of her she’d been denying all this time, sliding her hands over that marvelous, ever-roughened jaw of his to cup his beautiful face between her hands.

Her breath caught. She saw nothing but fire in his hot, sweet gaze, this stunning man whom she should never have met. Whom she should never have touched. Whose kiss weeks ago still worked in her like a fire she couldn’t stamp out and whose gorgeous male body, sculpted to impossible perfection, had been *right there within reach* on all those little holiday jaunts they’d taken, in all those rooms and tents they’d shared without ever sharing a bed.

She hadn’t touched him. She hadn’t dared. She didn’t know what would become of her if she followed that flame. She couldn’t imagine what waited for her on the other side—and she hadn’t known how to handle the fact she’d *wanted* things she’d never, ever wanted before, from anyone.

But tonight, she’d agreed to marry him. Tonight, they were in public, where it was safe. Where they could both wear the masks they preferred. Where there could be no real surrender to lick and scrape of all that fire inside of her.

Tonight, she felt as if she could dare anything. Even this. Even him.

Even the terrifying things she felt inside.

So Brittany slid forward and pressed her mouth to his.

It was better than she'd remembered—better than she'd dreamed. She tested the shape of his lips, shuddering at the warmth, the contact. He tilted his head to change the angle and took the kiss deeper, hotter.

His taste exploded through her, fine wine and devilishly perfect man.

God help her, but he was perfect.

Brittany kissed him as if fairy tales were real, and as if the two of them were, too. She kissed him as if they were nothing more than a man and a woman, and this kiss was all that mattered.

No kings, no strippers. No tabloid personas. No calculation whatsoever.

She couldn't seem to do anything but pour herself into him, no ice and nothing hidden or left back. No self-preservation at all.

Brittany kissed him as if she was falling in love with him, raw and wild and heedless, and her heart flipped over in her chest at the very thought.

And as if he knew it, Cairo pulled away. He brushed her hair back from her cheek, handling her as if she was infinitely precious to him. Something bloomed within her, warm and bright. Because she wanted that. She wanted to be precious.

To him.

"I promise you," he said, his voice husky with what she might have called a kind of pain, or maybe it was the honesty she'd asked for earlier, "you won't regret this."

"Neither will you," Brittany heard herself say, her voice as swollen as her lips, but a solemn vow even so.

It hung like that between them, shimmering and real.

And that was when the first paparazzo reached their table.

Six frantic and over-photographed weeks later, Brittany stood in a tiny stone chamber high in an ancient castle built into the side of the Italian coast, letting a set of smiling attendants lace her into her wedding gown. She kept her eyes trained on the tapestries that adorned the walls, all showing this or that medieval battle or glorified feast.

She tried to remind herself that this day, like all the conflicts and celebrations on display before her, would fade into blessed obscurity soon enough.

In five years, ten, a hundred, no one would care that Cairo Santa Domini was the first of his bloodline in three hundred years to marry outside the iconic cathedral that had stood for centuries in the Santa Dominian capital city, not far from the grand palace where his family once ruled. No one would care that he was—as a particularly vicious reporter had said to Brittany's face with obvious relish—polluting himself and the Santa Dominian line of ascension by consorting with her at all.

Time would pass. They would be messily and extravagantly divorced, as planned. They would make sure to drag it all out across the tabloids, the better to ensure the entire planet was heartily sick of them both. And then Brittany would fade off into obscurity and be remembered as nothing more than a tiny little footnote in the long, celebrated tale of Cairo's family that would end, ignominiously, with him.

It was too bad this particular footnote was fighting off a panic attack.

"Are you well, my lady?" one of the attendants asked

in heavily accented English as they finished the lacing. "You look pale."

"I'm fine," Brittany said, though her tongue felt strange in her mouth. She made herself smile. "I'm excited, that's all."

The women smiled back, the bustling and fussing continued, and then the church bells were ringing out the hour and it was really about to happen. In sixty short minutes she was going to walk outside to the chapel set high above the Mediterranean Sea and marry Cairo Santa Domini.

She dismissed the women from the room and stood there in the middle of it, fighting to keep her breath even and her eyes dry. Fighting to keep upright instead of sinking to her knees and staying there. Or worse, crawling into the four-poster bed that commanded the whole of one wall, hauling the covers up over her head and pretending she was the child she didn't think she'd ever been. Not really.

"Vanuatu," she muttered to herself. Fiercely. "Palm trees and white sands. Freedom and mai tais and life in sarongs."

Get your head into this, she ordered herself, in a pitiless sort of voice from down deep inside her that sounded a great deal like her harsh, bitter mother. *Right now. You have no other option.*

Brittany only realized her hands were clenched into fists when her fingers started to ache. She straightened them as the door to her chamber opened behind her, and then she smoothed the dress where it billowed out below her waist and—according to the mirror angled on its stand before her—made her look like a confection. She looked past it and out to the Italian hills that sloped toward the deep blue sea, dotted in marvelously colorful houses seemingly piled on top of each other while the staunch cypress trees stood like sentries beside them. She tried to breathe.

She kept trying.

"I'd like a few moments to myself," she managed to say after a moment, and was proud that her voice sounded much, much calmer than she felt.

"It is my role in life to disappoint you, I am afraid."

Cairo.

Of course.

Goose bumps swept over her, and she hoped he couldn't see them through the filmy, gossamer veil she wore pushed back to cascade over her shoulders toward the stone floor. His voice was richer than usual. Deeper and darker, and suddenly there was a lump in her throat that made it hard to swallow.

Then she turned to look at him and it was all much worse.

He was resplendent in white tie, lounging there in the doorway like a decidedly adult version of Prince Charming. The long tails of his morning coat did marvelous things to his lean, powerful frame, as if he'd been born to wear such formal clothes. A bubble of something giddy and inappropriate caught in her chest, and she had to swallow down near-hysterical laughter, because, of course, he had been. Bred for centuries on end to look nothing short of perfectly at his ease in attire most men found confining and strange.

"You are staring at my boutonniere as if you expect it to rise from my lapel and attack you," he said in his lazy, amused way, as he shut the heavy door behind him.

Brittany had never been a coward. She'd never had that option. And she didn't think she was one now, no matter how she felt inside. Still, the hardest thing she'd ever done in her life was to lift her gaze to meet his.

This glorious man. This would-be king. This inscrutable creature who was about to become her fourth husband.

Fourth, a small voice whispered deep inside of her,

with a certain feminine intuition she chose not to acknowledge, *and last.*

She shrugged that away, and the shiver of foreboding that crept down her spine, and let herself drink him in.

He looked exactly the way she'd expected Cairo Santa Domini would look on his wedding day. If, perhaps, more stunning. That careless dark hair of his was actually tamed. He'd even shaved his deliberately scruffy jaw, so he looked a bit less like a renegade than usual. He looked every inch the gleaming, impossibly wealthy and powerful royal he was.

And his eyes were more whiskey than caramel again. They seemed to see straight through her, pinning her to the wall like yet another decorative tapestry.

"What are you doing here?" she asked, and she hated that she sounded so much more stern and *bothered* by him than she'd intended. Or was wise. She cleared her throat. "Aren't you supposed to be waiting for me in the chapel?"

"It is not as if they can start without me." He eyed her, and she had no idea what he saw. No idea what that dark awareness that gleamed in his gaze was, only that it seemed to echo inside of her, growing bigger and wilder by the second. "I wanted to make certain you were not seized with any bright ideas about tossing yourself out the windows. A bridal suicide, while certainly bait for the tabloids, would simply mean I needed to start this process all over again. And I do hate to repeat myself."

"The papers we signed were clear. Death means no money at all. And if I abandon you at the altar I only get a quarter of what I would if I go through with it." She made herself shrug, as careless as he always was despite the fact she felt so soft and shivery. "It wouldn't be in my best interests to climb out the window, even if it wasn't a steep fall off a very long cliff to the sea."

Something occurred to her then, and gripped her so hard it was like a brutal fist around her heart.

"Why?" She didn't want to ask the next question, but she forced herself to do it anyway. "Have you changed your mind?"

Brittany understood far too many things in that airless, endless moment while she waited for his response. Too many things, too late. Too much she didn't want to admit, not even to herself.

This wedding was nothing like her others, two rushed courthouse visits and the small civil ceremony on the grounds of Jean Pierre's chateau that had been all about the gown she'd worn specifically to infuriate the old man's heirs. It had done its job. It had proclaimed her more Vegas showgirl than the solemn bride a man of Jean Pierre's standing should have been marrying, just as he'd wanted. She'd expected the dress for this even more dramatic performance today to be along those same lines. She'd been prepared for it, despite some drawings Cairo had showed her weeks ago that suggested a more classic approach.

But instead, the gown her attendants had dressed her in really was the one Cairo had showed her. Simple, elegant. It made her look like an actual, blue-blooded princess worthy of marrying a royal, not a tabloid sensation. Her breasts were not the main attraction. They weren't even on display. Her legs and thighs were not exposed every time she moved. Her veil, handed down in his family for generations and smuggled out of Santa Domini years ago, was almost as old as Cairo's title.

This wedding—this man—was nothing like the others.

And it made her feel things she'd never felt before. *He* did.

"I have not changed my mind," Cairo said.

His gaze was too bright and too assessing at once, and he seemed to fill the whole of the room, stone walls and the four-poster bed and ancient tapestries be damned. Then he stepped closer to her and that was worse. It was as if he took over the entire world while her heart simply hammered at her, telling her things about herself she didn't want to know.

Brittany had to order herself to stand still. To simply hold her ground, tilt her head back to keep her eyes on his face and keep herself from reacting when he reached over and took her hand in his. Idly, lazily, his fingers found the Heart of Santa Domini and moved the famous ring gently this way and that on her hand.

It was such a small, civilized sort of touch. It was so restrained, so conservative—nothing like that kiss in the burlesque club or the one staged for the slavering press in one of the finest restaurants in Paris. They were both wearing so many fine, carefully crafted clothes today, all of them formal and stuffy and exquisite. There was almost no flesh on display at all, in contrast to almost every other time they'd been together.

Not to mention, they were alone.

That word seemed to pound through her. *Alone.*

Maybe that was why his seemingly inconsequential touch *hummed* in her, stark and wildly electric, as if he'd done something far more wicked than take her hand in his. Something in her wished he had. She felt soft and desperate and deep inside her, high between her legs covered in yards and yards of shimmering white, something clenched hard and then pulsed.

She wished she wasn't a virgin. She wished she was as experienced as she pretended. Then she would know how to handle this. Then she would know what to do.

"Have you?" Cairo asked. Quiet and close, his attention trained on the ring.

"No," she said. It was not quite the set down she'd wanted to give. She was lucky she got the words out at all. And was that relief she saw chase across his gorgeous face? But that made no sense. It disappeared and she told herself she'd imagined it. "No, I haven't changed my mind."

There was no reason on earth that she should. Except, of course, that overwhelming sense of doom and ruin and longing and insane hope that was filling her nearly to bursting. She planned to keep right on ignoring the lot of it, straight on into the financial benefits of this arrangement that would have her feet sunk deep in the South Pacific sand within five years, tops.

All she had to do was keep herself from toppling over. Especially while Cairo was watching her…and touching her.

How could he manage to do this to her with so meaningless a touch?

"The guests have assembled," Cairo told her, as if none of this was getting to him. She envied him that. "The overbred scions from all the noble families in Europe or their more embarrassing relatives in their place, depending on how personally offended the sitting monarch is by my assorted shenanigans over the years."

"Of course, your friends and very distant family are here, as expected."

"In the sense that all of Europe's aristocratic families were related at some point or another?" He shrugged at that, though Brittany knew that he was listed in the lines of succession of at least five different kingdoms. "I would not call them my family. It would be rather presumptuous, among other things. But I cannot help noticing that your family are nowhere in evidence."

She wanted to tug her hand from his, but she suspected that would be too telling. Too revealing, when she already felt wide open and much too vulnerable, and this was the man who had showed her his real face in a restaurant in

Paris and then claimed she'd misread him. She needed to remember that. Cairo *wanted* these masks they wore.

She had no idea when she'd stopped wanting it, too.

"Mine weren't invited," she said. Abruptly.

Cairo's brows rose. He opened his mouth to say something that would no doubt cut her to the quick, and Brittany couldn't take it. She felt too exposed already. And suddenly she didn't care if he knew it. She pulled her hand back, but that didn't help. She could still feel that deceptively simple touch everywhere, as if he'd branded her.

"My family didn't sign up for this spectacle." She did nothing to ease that snap in her voice. "And it's not as if our marriage will last long anyway. It would take longer for them to get here than we'll stay together. Why bother?"

Brittany regretted her words almost the instant she said them. Cairo seemed turned to the same stone as the walls around them, and she knew, deep inside, that she'd offended him.

He looked away for a moment, toward the cliff and the sea and the Italian villages clinging to the hills in the distance as if the view could soothe him. When he looked back, there was a speculative expression on his face.

"You cannot be nervous, *cara*, can you?" He adjusted his crisp cuffs, one after the next, though his gaze never left hers. "This should be like falling off a log, as you Americans say, should it not? I am the wedding virgin here, after all, not you."

Later, she would reason that it was *that word*. She hadn't heard that ridiculous, archaic word in a long time, because who would bother to use it in the vicinity of such a well-known slut and, according to the more salacious papers, possible prostitute? It hardly came up in the strip clubs or dive bars where she used to spend all her time. Much less in Hollywood, the most virginless place she could imagine.

But here, now, in an old castle on the Italian coast, it hardly mattered *why* she flinched at the sound of the word. Only that she did, right there where Cairo could see her do it.

And then, much worse, she blushed.

Bright red and unmistakable.

She could feel the heat of it sweep over her, making her sweat and let out a harsh, loud breath. Her dress felt itchy all around her, suddenly. The combs that held her swept back veil felt prickly against her skull.

And worse than all of that was Cairo, who watched her with wholly undisguised fascination.

That and a very hungry sort of focus.

"Brittany," he said softly, so softly. "Do you have something you want to tell me?"

"No."

He laughed at her reply, but the way he watched her with those dark whiskey eyes of his only seemed to deepen. And then expand inside of her. "Can it be? Is it possible?"

The mortification and all that red heat seemed to roll tight inside of her, and she didn't know what to do with it. Only that if she didn't do *something*, she'd explode. She fought for some composure—but then came up hard against the far wall of the small, ancient room.

She hadn't even realized he'd been coming for her, or that she'd backed away from him. All the way across the room.

And now it was too late.

Cairo leaned in close as if he wanted to inhale the fine tremors that moved over her body, one after the next. Then he laid his hands on the cool stone wall, one palm on either side of her head, caging her where she stood.

"Stop lying to me," he ordered her, in that same quiet voice that did nothing to disguise the fact it was another steel-tipped royal command.

"We're about to get married for money so we can lead a tabloid life," she managed to bite out in some semblance of her usual composed, measured tone. "I thought lies were a given."

"Brittany," he said, and again, her name in that mouth of his *did things* to her she wished she could ignore, "are you the best-disguised and least likely virgin in the whole wide world?"

CHAPTER SIX

SOMETHING SHOOK THROUGH BRITTANY, long and deep.

She had to stop this. She had to distract him. She couldn't let him think she was an innocent, not today of all days. She didn't think she'd manage to survive it if he thought she was anything but the hard-shelled, cold-eyed creature she'd spent so many years pretending she was that she sometimes believed it herself.

Because she couldn't allow herself to be vulnerable. Not here. Not with him.

She didn't know how to handle the fact that Cairo was the only person she'd met in years who didn't see exactly what she wanted him to see when he looked at her.

Masks, she snapped at herself. *This relationship is about masks, not what's beneath them.*

"Of course I'm not a virgin," she said crisply, frowning at him. "Do people still use that word? Did it become the seventeenth century while I wasn't looking?"

He didn't look convinced. And Brittany knew, with every last fiber of her being, that she had to convince him he was mistaken and she had to do it *right this very minute* before it was too late—

Some part of her whispered that it already was.

That it had been too late from the moment she'd set foot in Monte Carlo.

And still Cairo looked at her in that deeply unsettling

way of his, as if he could see straight through to her battered old soul.

As if he already knew she was a virgin, whether she bothered to confirm it or not. As if a small fact she'd considered essentially meaningless for years told him everything he needed to know about her.

She couldn't have this. She couldn't let him think this, especially because it was true. It would ruin everything, she knew it.

"Impossible," she said when he didn't respond, but continued to watch her in that same considering way. It was much harder than it should have been to affect her trademark arch, amused voice. "Everyone knows I'm a whore, Cairo, and here's a news flash. They're not wrong."

"Including your own mother, I believe you mentioned."

Brittany would have said the names her mother had called her over time were a collection of very old scars set over wounds that had long since healed, and yet she ached when he said it. Still, she made herself smirk at him as if there were no scars, no ache, and never had been. Not beneath *her* mask.

"Especially my own mother."

That it wasn't strictly a lie gave her voice a little power, she thought. After all, some members of her family believed that listening to certain kinds of music rendered a woman instantly and irrevocably fallen. It was a slippery, easy slope from that to whoring about. Her mother had always been the first to say so, when it suited her.

Cairo shifted then. He left one hand on the wall as the other moved to trace a lazy pattern along the line of her jaw. Down the length of it, from near her ear to her chin. Then back again. And the look in his eyes was more than simply dangerous, then. It was possessive. Triumphant.

And very, very male.

Brittany felt that shaking thing inside of her again,

insistent and terrible. Some part of her wanted nothing more to surrender to it. To tell him the truth he'd already guessed. To stop lying about herself for one little second in all these years of living those lies to the hilt.

Just here. Just to him. Just to the only man whose kiss had made her feel like a woman, not a means to an end.

But that was insanity. That bordered on *intimate* and she knew better than to risk such a thing. Not with *Cairo Santa Domini*, in the name of all that was holy, given his version of intimacy likely involved cutting down to three orgies a week from seven.

What the hell was she thinking?

She blamed the dress. The elegant princess dress that gave a woman *ideas*, even a woman who should know better. The dress that looked as if it had fallen from the pages of a fairy tale and made even a trailer-park Cinderella like Brittany imagine princes were real and charming and right here in front of her at last.

Life had taught her better than that. Over and over again.

So she smiled at Cairo, suggestively and wickedly. She reached up and covered the hand he held to her cheek with hers, and arched herself into him. She pressed her breasts against his chest and she tilted back her head to keep her gaze on his, and she did her best to ignore the way those things made the fire inside her sear through her.

"I can play a virgin if you want me to," she murmured, her voice sultry. "Why am I not surprised that the most famous playboy in Europe likes a little role play?"

That hot blaze in his eyes deepened. The air between them seemed to pull tight, as if something huge clenched around her, then squeezed. Hard.

"Are we playing?" he asked quietly.

"A marriage like this is nothing but a game." Brittany made herself pout at him when he only continued to stare down at her, as if he really was trying to see inside of her. He shifted, dragging his chest against hers so that tendrils of flame curled through her and made it hard not to squirm where she stood. And harder still to remember she was supposed to be acting. "Why not take it into bed as well?"

"You told me there was to be no sex in this marriage." His gaze was on her mouth. Her heart pounded hard, like a sledgehammer.

"You told me that wasn't your style," she countered.

She didn't know when she noticed that he'd angled his torso into her. That he was holding her there against the wall that easily, and Brittany knew she should have hated it. She should have felt caught. Captured. *Compromised.*

She didn't.

His eyes glowed that dark amber that made her chest feel tight, and she couldn't seem to pull in a full breath to save her life. His palm was surprisingly hard and warm against her cheek. She could feel it in her toes. His chest pressed against hers and made her breasts ache, the peaks pinching into hard points. And that beautiful mouth of his was set in a stern, resolute line that made something giddy and wild race through her, then coil tight low in her belly.

"I already told you I want to be inside you, Brittany," he told her, and it had the ring of a vow. Of something stitched together, need and command as one, and a red hot punch straight to that place that already melted for him. "That hasn't changed."

She rotated her hips, pulling him closer to her, and then she slid both of her hands around his neck. Her pulse was a riot, hammering through her veins and striking rapid blows in her temples, her throat, her wrists. And deep between her legs, where she ached and melted and ached some more.

And Brittany forgot that she was playing a role. She forgot everything but the fact she wanted him, as extraordinary as that was. *She wanted him.* And the whole world already thought he'd had her a million times, so who was she saving herself for if not this curious man who got beneath her skin as no one else ever had?

"Then why aren't you?" she asked. Cairo seemed to freeze there before her, save the hand that had gripped her jaw. He dropped it then, but his eyes stayed locked to hers. "Why aren't you inside me, when you are renowned the world over for your inability to keep it in your own trousers? Why have we spent our entire relationship so chastely and demurely?" She laughed at that, because she didn't know the answer herself when the only thing inside her was this edgy, delirious need. "Or is this terrible reputation of yours no more than the fevered imaginings of an overworked publicist somewhere?"

His gaze took on a light she'd never seen before, but she felt it. God help her, but she felt it, deep inside of her, where she was nothing but slippery longing and very bad ideas.

"Why don't we find out?" he murmured, his voice like silk.

Silk and danger and too much heat besides.

He shifted again, then. He reached down between them and began pulling up her heavy white skirt, never moving that demanding gaze of his from hers.

Brittany couldn't have said a word if she'd tried.

She didn't try.

And this time, when he traced patterns over the top of one thigh and then dipped into the valley between her legs, he didn't stop there. He found the silken panties she wore and smoothed his way beneath them, and then it was happening. It was really happening.

He was touching her where no one else had ever touched her.

Him.

Cairo.

He made a low, approving noise that rolled over her like another caress, as if finding her heat made him feel as raw as she did, and she surrendered herself all over again.

She had the distant thought that she always would.

Cairo stroked her tender flesh with his fingers, his eyes glittering darkly as her lips parted. Brittany did nothing—could do nothing—but lean back against the wall. And die from the pleasure of his touch, over and over and over. And let her hips rise to meet him with every slippery, decadent stroke, as if she was learning how to dance for the very first time.

As if he was teaching her the steps to the most perfect dance of all.

"It almost feels as if I know what I'm doing," he murmured, his voice a low, throbbing thing that mixed in with the slick, delicious movement of his hand, there against an old castle wall. "I can almost imagine no publicist has been involved in the creation of my reputation. What do you think?"

But everything else was lost in that fire he built in her and she couldn't respond. She wasn't sure she would have responded if she could. Not when she could disappear into the sweet glory of his touch instead.

And that was when he found the center of her need. He pressed against it once, then again, making her moan out loud. She told herself an experienced woman wouldn't react the way she did—but she couldn't seem to help herself, not when he ground his hand against her.

"Let's consider this an object lesson," Cairo murmured, dropping his head beside hers, his breath against her neck. "You have a habit of saying things no other person alive would dare say to me. Perhaps I have finally found the appropriate way to respond."

He twisted his wrist, plunging a finger deep inside her

molten heat while the rest of his hand rocked hard against the place where she ached the most.

It was an invasion. *It was perfect.*

He did it again, then again, then added a second finger and did it once more.

And Brittany simply…broke apart.

She shook and she shattered, and she fell into a thousand pieces right there in her wedding dress with her fingers dug deep into his arms, and the only thing she knew in all the world was his hard hand and his rough voice at her ear. She might have fallen apart forever, tumbling this way and that into a million little shards of who she'd been. She felt as if she had.

And when she came back to herself she was slumped against the smooth wall and the only thing holding her up was the arm she hadn't realized Cairo had put around her waist, securing her there against him.

He was watching her closely when she finally focused on him again, with an expression she'd never seen on his royal face before. Hard and solemn at once, and lit from within with a kind of hunger that made her clench tight all over again, against the fingers she could still feel inside of her.

Inside of her. Brittany let loose a shudder, low and deep, through a brand-new lick of need and heat.

Cairo smiled at that. He took his time pulling his hand away. He smoothed the silken fabric over her heat and then he drew his hand away entirely, letting the heavy wedding dress fall back into place to cover her weak knees and legs.

As if none of it had happened, when she was still soft and soaked and trembling.

"Brittany," he began, as if that wasn't the same sensual hunger that stormed through her turning his gorgeous face stark.

And something surged in her then, shocking her back

from that syrupy sweet place he'd thrown her into so easily, so expertly. Some kind of heightened awareness, or desperation. She didn't know what it was, she only knew with every inch of her body that she had to act instantly or lose everything.

"Is that it?" she asked, and she'd never sounded more bored. She heaved a sigh and pushed away from him, taking advantage of the look of arrogant astonishment on his face to swish her great skirts around him and start toward the other side of the room. "Clueless teenagers commit more interesting sins while fully clothed in the hallways of their high schools. I expected a little more finesse from a man who calls himself a king."

"Finesse," he repeated, as if he was unfamiliar with the word, and he sounded far closer to her than she'd expected. And far more cutting. Every hair on the back of her neck stood, but she didn't turn around. "The excitement of our wedding day must be playing havoc with my hearing. I just imagined you questioned my *finesse* mere seconds after you climaxed in my hands. Surely not."

She turned around then and her stomach flipped over, because he was *right there.*

He kept coming. Brittany decided to stop moving and stood there at the foot of the four-poster bed, trying to exude bored experience while her knees still felt like jelly.

"It's okay," she murmured, as insincerely as possible. She rolled her eyes. "I'm sure you're great."

His head tilted slightly to one side and the way he smiled then, slow and hard, made her think of a wolf.

"Oh, I am at that." Cairo reached over and ran a finger down the length of her hair, then tugged on the end. Once, then again. Not precisely hard—and yet that small hint of sharpness seemed to rebound through her overheated body, blooming into something much hotter and more intense in the place that still ached for him the most. "But by all means, *cara*, do not take my word for it."

And then he bent down and swept her up off her feet, huge dress and veil and all, and tossed her onto the bed.

Cairo hardly let himself think.

She landed on the bed with a soft exhalation and then he was there with her, levering himself above her and holding himself up on his elbows.

"Cairo—"

"Quiet, *cara.* Allow me to meet the challenge you issued, if you please."

His voice was a lash of command. He hardly recognized it. But that didn't seem to matter. Nothing seemed to matter except this woman dressed in white, with those dark eyes still so hot and wild and all for him. This woman who would shortly be his wife. *My wife*, he repeated, and the words seemed to reverberate inside of him, growing so big and so loud they filled him up—then crowded out everything else.

The world. His sense. *Everything.*

Cairo didn't care. He traced her lips with his fingers and hoped she could taste her own need when he did. She flushed that intoxicating red again, and it made him feel dizzy. It made a beast he hadn't known that lurked so deep inside him roar.

For once in his life, he didn't calculate the outcome of this encounter or worry about his performance. He'd left that somewhere behind them on the stone floor, tangled up in those abandoned little moans she'd made that left him so hard and so wild for her he ached.

He ached.

"Cairo," she said again, and this time her voice was little more than a whisper. But he recognized the heat in it. The impossible fire that burned in him, too.

He forgot how they'd come to be here. He only knew that finally, *finally*, Brittany was beneath him. *Where she belonged*, that beast in him growled.

What else could possibly matter?

He reached between them and pulled her dress up and out of his way. She made a soft, high sound, but when their gazes clashed she pulled her lower lip between her teeth. Then rocked her hips against him as he settled himself between her soft, leanly muscled thighs in wordless welcome.

God help him, but she was perfect.

He leaned in close and took her mouth with his, with all the desperate ruthlessness of a man about to explode. Her taste washed through him, sweet woman and all Brittany. He lost himself in the sheer perfection of it. He tasted her again and again, then angled his head for a hotter, slicker fit and did it all over again.

She lifted herself to meet him, her tongue meeting his and then driving him slowly, inevitably, gloriously insane.

Cairo had been acting a part for a long time. He'd pretended to be lost in a thousand kisses, usually for the benefit of the cameras that always waited nearby. But there were no cameras here and the longer he indulged himself in this woman, the more he forgot he'd ever treated a kiss like a stage.

This time, he really was lost.

He wanted her naked. He wanted her without a stitch of clothing on her perfect, delectable body, spread out before him like the feast she was. He wanted to take his time. He wanted to wallow in sensation, bathe in passion, throw himself completely into this woman and never come up for air—

But the bodice stopped him. It was a piece of understated elegance, embroidered and close-fitting, and it penetrated the fist of need that had him locked in its grip.

Just enough to remember that there were people waiting. That there were other things he needed to do to Brittany today, like marry her.

He could think of only one thing he wanted more, just then.

He deepened the kiss. His mouth mated with hers, taking her and taunting her. Making her flush and buck against him, her hands clutching at him and urging him on.

"Are you ready?" he asked her.

"I've been ready for weeks," she retorted, as he should have expected.

Cairo reached down between them and worked at his trousers, then smoothed his hand back beneath her silken panties, still beautifully damp from before. She was still molten hot and mind-numbingly soft, and she was *his*.

He'd been waiting for this moment since the moment he'd seen her picture, so long ago now. He'd longed for this since the night they'd met in Monte Carlo. He'd imagined this a thousand different ways since she'd walked out on him that night and left him to stew in his own wild need.

Cairo had never wanted another woman more.

He lined himself up with her slick, ready entrance *at last*, then thrust himself home.

It hurt.

He was huge and hard and so deep inside her, and the sensation that burst within her was too much. *Too much.*

Brittany went stiff, unconsciously slamming her hands in fists against his chest, and Cairo froze.

She'd imagined she could play it off. She'd been so sure that all her years of dancing would have loosened her up, made this a nonissue, the way so many of the other girls had claimed it had for them. She'd wanted him so much that she'd been positive she could simply throw herself into this thing without him pausing or even noticing that it was her first time.

But his eyes were dark and faintly accusing as they met hers now. His beautiful face was taut. He held himself very, very still above her, but there was no mistaking the steel length of him still sunk deep inside her, or the utter foreignness of the big, hard, decidedly male body nestled tight between her thighs.

He was stretching her. He was inside her and he was stretching her and she could *feel him* everywhere. With every shuddering breath she took.

But far worse than that, he had definitely noticed.

Brittany felt tears pool in the corners of her eyes, when she hadn't *cried* in longer than she could remember, and she couldn't believe she felt so *undone.*

"Do you care to explain this turn of events?" Cairo asked, conversationally, which only made that particular hot gleam in his eyes seem more dangerous.

She tried to blink back the tears in her eyes and swallow down that lump in her throat, but only made a snuffling sort of sound instead. She *snuffled.* She was flat on her back in the most beautiful wedding dress she'd ever seen, His Serene Grace the Archduke Felipe Skander Cairo of Santa Domini braced above her and deep *inside* her, no longer a virgin no matter what happened next if she understood the mechanics of these things correctly, and she'd *snuffled.*

Like some kind of animal.

"Do not cry," he ordered her. His gaze gentled as it met hers and it was astonishing how comforting Brittany found that. "Don't you dare cry, *tesorina.* You have lived through far worse things than me, I am confident."

A moment ago she'd had a sob inside her chest, so big she'd been afraid it would burst straight out through her ribs like some kind of alien creature and engulf them both, and now she wanted to laugh. She loosened the fists she still had clenched against him, uncurling her fingers and then smoothing them over the elegant morning coat he wore. Almost as if she was comforting *him.*

She opted not to analyze that.

"I haven't yet determined whether or not I'll live through this," she pointed out after a moment, and though her voice was thicker than normal, there were no tears in it.

She could feel him, hard and so astonishingly hot, still wedged deep inside her. The very thought of it made her a little bit breathless, and then there was how it *felt*. Or maybe it was just him, braced above her so that thick hair of his fell down his forehead the way it always did. But there were still no tears. And then his mouth curved, and Brittany couldn't imagine why she'd ever felt like crying.

Cairo lowered himself to his elbows and cradled her face in his hands. It made him move the slightest bit inside of her, the faintest bit of friction where she was nothing but tender and new and scared, and it hurt again. She stiffened in the same instant she recognized that the pain was far less than before.

"You will live," he assured her. He held himself still again. "I promise."

He was heavy and hard, and her dancer's thighs, which she'd thought could handle any amount of stretching, felt… different. They almost ached from this strange position, pressed down and wide open by another person so much larger and more solidly muscular than she was. Still, it wasn't a painful ache. Not quite.

"It is your maidenly virtue that we must mourn here today," Cairo continued, sounding almost as lazy as he normally did, despite that caramel gleam in his dark eyes. "That and your penchant to lie directly to my face are two topics I imagine we will spend some time discussing in the days to come."

"Let's not get carried away." She frowned at him. "I might not have had sex before, but that doesn't make me—"

"A virgin? I think you'll find that is, in fact, the textbook definition."

"Virtuous." Her frown deepened. "I haven't been remotely virtuous since I was a kid and I was never much of a maiden, either. I have three husbands who would agree."

"Three husbands, yes." His gaze held hers, hot and gleaming, and he moved then. A simple little slide. An adjustment, nothing more, and it made her breath catch as she clutched at him. But it didn't hurt. Not at all, this time. "But no one has ever been here but me."

She scowled at him.

"I will take that as the confirmation I do not actually require," he murmured.

He pulled her closer to him, and Brittany was astounded to feel herself begin to melt all around him again. That look in his eyes changed again, and this time, the flush she felt was from something that felt a great deal like shame.

"You should have told me." Cairo's voice was reproving, and there was that edge to it she didn't quite understand. Once again, she had the wild notion she was looking at a Cairo no one else had ever seen, this man who looked at her with something akin to tenderness in his gaze. Deep inside, she trembled. "I did not wish to hurt you. I am not quite that monstrous. Not quite."

"I…" This was so far outside her experience. She didn't know what to do, what to say. She'd never *felt* so many things at once, physical sensation mixed with a flash flood of emotion, and all the while Cairo simply held himself there. Not hurting her. Not rushing her. Not leaving her. As if he could stay like that forever. "I didn't want you to know."

"Because you thought I would mind?" he asked, and though his voice was mild enough she thought she heard an edge in it. He still didn't move. "Or because you thought it would give you better leverage to throw your virginity at the highest title in your vicinity?"

She tipped her chin up as if she wanted to fight him for saying that. Maybe she did. Or maybe that was her only defense when he accused her of something so outside her imagining that she felt lacerated.

"I can't imagine a single person alive who would imagine that Cairo Santa Domini, patron saint of the lascivious, would have the slightest interest in whether or not someone was a virgin. You are whatever the opposite of a virgin is. Times a million."

His dark eyes gleamed. "As it turns out, I find myself deeply interested and also deep inside you. Perhaps they are related states."

She tilted her head back to glare at him more fully. "If I'd known the possibility of a truly white wedding mattered to you, because you are apparently a giant cliché masquerading as a man, I would have made certain to demand more money for going through with it." Her voice was as icy as possible, and yet even she could hear she sounded much too rough. And that it was far too revealing. She soldiered on, "And if I'd known you were a walking caveman, I would have turned you down the way I wanted to do from the start, no matter how many provocative pictures you sold to the tabloids."

"I am a king, Brittany."

That rang out between them, and she thought she saw something like amazement on his face for a moment, though he blinked it away. He seemed to get harder, bigger. Propped over her like that, still lodged inside of her, he became the whole world.

And Brittany found she couldn't seem to say another word.

"Not a cliché, not a caveman, not common in any way," he told her, in that same quietly ringing tone. "And I may not have a kingdom or the subjects I deserve, but I will have a wife before this day is done. I will have you. Like this. As long as we are together, I will have you exactly like this."

Cairo said it as if they stood at the altar already and these were the promises he was making to bind them together. She shook again, deep inside. Then, following an urge she didn't entirely understand, she moved her hips. She rocked them against his. His eyes darkened. And she pulled in a breath.

Because that didn't hurt at all. In fact, it felt…interesting.

"And whatever games we play in public, Brittany, what we do in private is ours. More specifically, mine."

"Cairo," she whispered. "I think I want you to start moving now."

Something flared in his gaze then, a deep, male satisfaction and that same hunger she recognized.

"Your wish is my command, *tesorina*," he told her. "But first you must say it."

"What do you want me to say?" She rocked against him again, against that impossible length of his buried so deep inside her, and shivered when sensation swirled through her. Lighting her up from the tips of her ears to the hard points of her nipples, past the molten place where they were connected, down into the toes that curled in the delicate shoes she still wore.

"Tell me," he urged her, and he pulled back then. Slowly. Slowly and steadily, inch by inch, and it made Brittany flush. Then try to meet him when he reversed himself and sank back into her. Deep and sure. "Tell me that in this, I am your king if no one else's. That here, you are mine."

She would have told him absolutely anything just then. Anything at all.

"Yours," she agreed, her head moving against the bed as he repeated that luxurious slide. Even more intense, delicious sensations coiled in her and flashed like wildfire through her entire body. Again and again. "I'm all yours."

"You have no idea how true that is, *tesorina mia*," Cairo muttered, dark and urgent, and then he really began to move.

And Brittany simply surrendered herself into a mass of pure sensation.

Cairo set a lazy, easy pace, and he encouraged her to meet him. Brittany moved her hips as he directed her, growing bolder with each stroke until she wrapped her legs around his hips.

He built the fire between them high and bright and so intense she didn't see how anyone could live through it. She also didn't care. He thrust harder, deeper, and she gloried in it. In him. As if she'd spent her whole life searching for this. As if this, right here, was exactly where she was meant to be.

As if her body knew things her mind didn't want to examine.

Still, he urged her on. Still, he swept her along with him, until she was hovering on another precarious cliff of his making.

"I can't…" she whispered.

"But you will," he replied, fierce and sure. "For me."

He reached between them and stroked her where she needed him the most. Brittany tipped her head back and gripped him tight as he pounded into her. Again and again—

Until finally, she hurtled off into nothingness, breaking apart into too many scattered little bits to name.

And this time, he called out her name and followed her right over that edge.

She had the vague notion they floated out in that silken, beautiful darkness together for a very long time. It could have been years.

But Cairo was already up and moving when she finally thudded back into her own skin and opened her eyes again.

"Stay where you are," he told her, in that bossy tone of voice she thought she really ought to object to.

But she didn't say a word. Nor did she move. She felt loose and lazy as she lay there on the old four-poster bed. There were all manner of thoughts and problems and issues hovering there, waiting for her to acknowledge them, but she ignored them. She listened to the cries of the seabirds on the other side of the windows instead, wafting in on the sweet summer breeze. She felt the sunlight dance over her face. She imagined she could hear the sea against the rocks, far below.

She felt bright and sunny straight through, as if she could drift away into the blue sky forever.

Cairo came back to her then, and she blinked, because he looked immaculate as he stood there at the foot of the bed. Not a wrinkle, or a hair out of place. As if none of this had happened when she could still feel him between her legs, where she was deliciously tender. She knew that should have bothered her. It should have done *something* other than make her shudder with a little more of that heat. He moved to put a hand on her belly and she shivered at his touch, then again when he used the cloth in his other hand to tend to her.

"You did not bleed much," he told her matter-of-factly, and she flushed at that. As if the words were more intimate than the act they'd shared. He tucked the cloth into her panties, pulled them back into place over her hips and then helped her to her feet, smoothing her dress down around her as she stood. "Leave that there until just before you walk down the aisle."

"What?" She wanted the floor to swallow her whole. She stared at the stones, willing it to do just that. "I don't want to talk about this with you."

"Brittany." She couldn't help but obey him when he used that voice, but he took her chin in his hand to make certain. "You are wearing a very white dress and you will be standing in it before a large congregation and a great many cameras. This is no time for modesty."

She pulled away then and stepped around him, amazed that her legs held her up when she felt as if she'd been swept away. As if she wasn't entirely herself anymore.

As if the mask she'd worn all her life had shattered, leaving her with nowhere to hide.

"This was a mistake," she said, sounding stilted to her own ears. "That shouldn't have happened."

It took everything she had to pull herself together. To lift her chin, run her hands over her veil, manage to smooth out her expression. She moved to the mirror and was as amazed as she was oddly disappointed that she looked exactly the same. The same as she had before he'd come into this room and more, wholly unruffled. As if nothing had happened between them but a little chat, like all the other little chats they'd had over the past weeks. All she needed to do was reapply her lipstick and no one would ever be the wiser.

She decided to take that as a sign. A portent, even.

"That will never happen again," she told him, raising her gaze to meet his in the mirror.

He moved to stand directly behind her, and her body knew him. It ached for him. She felt herself soften, everywhere, and had no idea what to do about it. As if he knew it simply by looking at her, Cairo smiled. He slid his hand around to hold her there before him, stretching his palm against the tight waist of her gown.

She felt the heat of it everywhere, like a promise. She wanted to lean into it, into him. She would never know how she kept herself from doing it. How she kept her spine straight and her knees locked.

"You are going to marry me in approximately five minutes," Cairo told her, and she couldn't help but remember the way he'd said "I am a king," as if he'd never said such a thing out loud before. She could hear the echo of it again now, and more, feel it deep inside her. Like a command from on high. "You are going to remember what happened here with every step you take down that aisle. I have no intention of a carrying on a sexless marriage, Brittany. Certainly not with a woman who wants me as badly as you do. Almost as badly as I want you."

"I..."

But she didn't know what she meant to say. What she could say, when every last cell in her body wanted nothing more than to throw herself back onto that bed again. To tear off her clothes and all of his and actually explore him this time. Then lose herself in all that marvelous shattering all over again. Right here, right now, and who cared how many noble personages waited for them below?

"I was always planning to seduce you, Brittany," Cairo told her as he pulled his arm from around her body. He righted her when she started to slump over because her knees really weren't working, and she flushed at his touch all over again. His firm lips moved into that small curve that set off explosions all through her. "Now I will simply take comfort in the fact that inevitably, I will ruin you for all other men. I likely already have. What a great pity."

"That's a lovely sentiment," she managed to say, trying desperately to sound as composed and as dry as she wished she was. "I'm signing up to be your wife for a little while, not become your…"

She faltered, not knowing what word to use. What this was, what she was.

Or, worse, what she wanted to be. With him. For him. Much less for herself.

Cairo smiled at her then, and this time, it reached his eyes. And it was as lethal to her as the way he'd touched her, as the way he'd moved inside her, as the way he'd made her feel. It was almost too much to bear, too bright and too perfect, like the impossible Italian summer on the other side of the window.

He was her ruin made real and today she'd ensured it. She felt something inside her crack wide open and she was terribly afraid it would suck her in and destroy her right then and there, whatever it was. It felt that brutal and that permanent.

The trouble was, some part of her wanted to see what would happen. Some part of her imagined the wreck of it—of this—would be worth it, no matter what came after.

"Don't worry," Cairo told her, as if he felt it, too, that great, wide, open thing that was already changing everything. As if he knew exactly what it was and what it meant. As if this was as real as it felt—as real as that silly, fairy-tale-headed fool inside of her wanted it to be. "You will be both. My wife, yes. My countryless queen in all your glory. But most of all, Brittany, you will be mine. Do you not understand? You already are."

CHAPTER SEVEN

THE LAST OF the Santa Dominis married his stripper bride in a private chapel that dated back to the Italian Renaissance, the first of his family to marry in a place other than the Grand Cathedral in Santa Domini's capital in centuries.

Three whole centuries, to be exact.

As the old hymns were sung and the old words intoned, Cairo stood at an altar his ancestors had built with a woman for whom he felt entirely too many complicated things to name and found it hard to remember that he was baiting a trap. It was much too difficult to focus on the real purpose of this performance.

Because all he could think of, all he could see, all he could concentrate on was Brittany.

Who had somehow seen beneath every last mask he wore. And was already his.

Princes and counts and the assorted minor arcana of Europe sat in the pews arranged behind him, yet all Cairo could think about was the fact of her innocence and his taking of it. Her sweet heat and her addictive taste. The untutored rawness of the way she'd moved beneath him and the greedy little sounds she'd made as she'd found her release. He had to shift slightly as he stood to mask his body's response to the onslaught of memory, lest he appall the gathered throng of European nobles even more than he already had by making them bear witness to this ceremony in the first place.

Pay attention to the game, you fool, he ordered himself as the priest waved his hands over his bride's elegantly veiled head and intoned sacred words down the length of the chapel.

He was making this woman his in every conceivable way today, and despite the niggling sense that he was forgetting something critical, he exulted in it. If was up to him, he thought, he'd lock her up somewhere far away and out of the public eye, and indulge himself in her forever.

But that, of course, was not the game they played. No matter that she wasn't at all the practiced trollop she'd pretended she was for years. Nobody alive could possibly know that except Cairo—and in any case, it changed nothing.

The fact he felt he could show her the truth in him didn't mean he should, or that it altered the course they'd set out. It only made him hate himself that much more.

"I don't understand," Brittany had said weeks ago. It had been a few days after their engagement dinner. Enterprising paparazzi were attempting to scale the gates of his Parisian residence and the sketches he'd commissioned from his preferred Italian dressmaker had been spread out between them on the coffee table in one of his salons. "This looks like something a proper English princess would wear. I assumed we'd be taking the loud and tacky route."

"Everyone will be expecting that, of course." He'd eyed her, all copper fire and that distance in her gaze. He'd had the fleeting notion she'd been protecting herself—but he'd dismissed it. Why should she need protection? She was the one marrying up. "I have something else in mind."

A different sort of color bloomed high on her lovely cheeks, his mother's ring gleamed on her finger and it was a dangerous game he'd been playing. He'd known that all along, but perhaps never so keenly as in that moment.

"I don't understand." He'd had the impression she'd thought about how to respond. Her words were too precise. "I thought the point was to horrify the entire world with your marriage to a bargain-basement upstart like me."

"I want something slightly more complicated than a circus of a ceremony and a parade of bad taste," he'd said quietly. "That would be an obvious stunt. And not only because that was how you did it the last time you married above your station."

There had been a hint of misery in her dark hazel gaze. Then she'd blinked it away and lifted her chin, and he'd wondered if he'd only wanted that kind of reaction from her. If that was why he kept baiting her.

If he'd *wanted* her to feel all the things he was terribly afraid he felt himself.

"You want them to pity you," Brittany had said softly.

She hadn't met his gaze then. The iconic ring he'd slid onto her finger so recently had seemed to dance in the Parisian morning light between them, hoarding the sunshine and then sending it cartwheeling across the room.

Like joy, he'd thought. Not that he would know.

Brittany had still been talking. "You want them to think you believe that the sheer force of your feelings for me makes me somehow appropriate. You want to present a sow's ear all dressed up like a silk purse and pretend you can't tell the difference. You want them to laugh at you. At me."

She'd met his gaze then and it had taken everything he had to keep from flinching. He, who had never so much as blinked at all the tawdry things he'd done in his lifetime. He, who had always known precisely what his mission was and how best to achieve it, no matter how many reports he received that the general's health continued to decline.

"I do," he'd said, and he'd pretended that he hadn't seen

her pretty eyes go darker at that. Or, more to the point, he'd pretended he didn't care.

He said the same words now.

His voice was strong and sure to carry throughout the chapel and dispel any possible doubt that he was marrying this woman—*his woman.* He kept his fingers clasped tight around hers. And he waited.

But it wasn't until she replied in kind, sending relief arrowing through him, that Cairo realized he hadn't known what she'd say. Some part of him had truly believed that Brittany might change her mind at the last moment and take off running, like some captured bride of old. Another part of him wouldn't have blamed her if she had.

Here in this church, as he slid a new ring onto her finger to proclaim her his without any doubt or wiggle room, Cairo found absolutely nothing amusing about the idea of Brittany anywhere but here. With him.

The whole world thought they knew her, but only he did.

She was his in every possible way.

"You may kiss the bride," the priest intoned.

Cairo wanted to do a great deal more than simply kiss her.

But this was a stage, he reminded himself. This was an act. This was his opportunity to paint himself the besotted fool for the cameras.

He told himself he was a lucky man, indeed, that it was so easy.

Brittany tilted her face up to his, her pretty eyes darker than usual. He wanted that to be evidence. He wanted her to be as swept away in this as he was. He hated that he couldn't quite tell how much of her was real and how much of her was a performance.

It had been different up in that old stone chamber. When he'd been able to feel the truth of her, of them, in the way she shook apart in his hands and then again beneath him. When he'd ridden them both into all that glorious fire and let them burn and burn and burn.

God, how he wanted to do it again.

He pressed his mouth to hers. He felt her tremble against him when he deepened the kiss, holding her against him a beat or two longer than was strictly polite, and he saw the vulnerable cast to her temptation of a mouth when he finally released her.

She was thinking about what had happened between them, too. About him sunk deep inside her and her legs wrapped around him. He knew it as well as he knew his own name.

"Next time," she murmured, right there against his lips, "why don't you brand me with your initials instead? Or perhaps urinate in a circle around me, like a dog?"

"Is that a request?" he asked, in a low voice pitched for her ears alone. "Or a dare?"

And then he pulled back and presented her to the assembled crowd, before she could answer back in her usual tart way. His queen at last, and who cared what those vultures thought of her?

He knew what he thought: that his honeymoon couldn't come fast enough, because one taste of her wasn't nearly enough.

Cairo couldn't remember ever wanting a woman the way he wanted this one. *His wife*, he thought as they made their way down the chapel's long aisle and then stepped out into the exuberant Italian sunshine. It was such a small word, and yet he couldn't seem to process it. *His wife.*

There was only one other thing in all the world he'd ever wanted so badly it had consumed him whole. Thinking of his lost kingdom as they moved, Cairo thought he should be ashamed that he'd lost sight of it for even a moment. No matter how his new queen's smile caught the sun and made the whole world a little brighter all around her as they walked from the chapel. The wedding breakfast that waited for them, arranged in artistically laden long tables in the old castle keep, was not the place to forget who he was or the role he needed to play here.

Because it had never been more crucial to keep up his usual act than it was today.

"I never thought I'd see the day," one of his supposed best and oldest friends said with an entirely feigned congratulatory grin, slinging his arm over Cairo's shoulders in a show of his usual drunkenness as Cairo made his rounds sometime later. Cairo could see right through it, but then, there wasn't much of Harry Marbury—a man constructed of as many impeccably pedigreed English forebears as cast-off morals—that wasn't entirely transparent. "It's not as if you must marry to secure the kingdom, Cairo. It's been lost all your life and no matter those rumors that the old soldier is on his last legs. What *is* this preposterous wedding all about?"

"We all must fall in our time," Cairo replied lazily, as if mention of the general didn't scrape at him. And he hated himself when he continued, as he knew he must. "Better to cushion that landing in a woman who knows her way around a stripper pole, in my opinion."

"One does not marry the trash, friend," Harry said, laughing in his condescending way—and raising his voice just enough that it carried across the gathering and over to where Brittany stood with that fake smile on her face. Cairo saw her stiffen and he hated all of this. These lies, these performances, when what had happened between them had been real. Raw and real and entirely theirs. The most real and unscripted he thought he'd ever been in his life. "One uses it and then one's servants puts it out. In bins, I'm told."

Cairo would never know how he managed to keep himself from murdering the man—his supposed oldest, dearest friend—with his own two hands just then, right where they stood in the medieval courtyard of the old castle keep.

But he didn't, because this was exactly what he'd wanted. What he'd gone to such great lengths to make happen, precisely like this. He had no one to blame but himself if he didn't like how it felt now.

Now that she was his wife. His exiled queen.

His, damn it.

That was the part that mattered. That and the headlines Harry's little comment would likely generate from all the hangers-on that Cairo knew full well spent half their time in his presence texting the tabloids with choice snippets that usually bred headlines. And that was why Cairo laughed indulgently and clapped Harry on the back as if he'd told a rousing great joke instead of exterminating him like the cockroach he was.

You deserve a medal of valor for letting him live, he told himself grimly as he smiled and laughed and encouraged all these parasites to pity him as the reception wore on. Just as he'd planned.

Though it was hard to mind any of that when he had Brittany in his arms again.

She tilted her head back as they danced together for the first time as husband and wife, exiled king and nominal queen, smiling up at him for the benefit of the crowd.

"You look as if you are head over heels for me," he told her, and tried to sound as if he was chiding her when all he could think about was keeping his hands where they belonged. Instead of where he longed to put them. He was sure everyone could see it and with it, his real face. His true self. And yet all he wanted to do was continue to gaze down at her. "The papers will not know whether to call you smitten or materialistic."

"It must be the romance of the day," she said dryly. "It's

going to my head. Next thing you know I'll be reciting poetry and telling all the papers it was love at first sight, right there in that nightclub in the sewers of Paris where they think we met."

Two things happened then, in an instant.

First, a hard kick in the vicinity of Cairo's chest, making him clasp Brittany tighter as he fought it off. He tried to tell himself he didn't know what it was—but he did. Of course he did. Anticipation, desire… As if he wanted this to be real. As if he wanted this to be the mad, epic romance they were pretending it was.

As if it already was.

But that wasn't possible. He knew that as well as he knew his own, cursed name.

Because the second thing that happened was a vicious punch, straight to the gut. Cairo knew what happened when love was involved. He'd lived it. He was still living it. Grief and horror and crushing, interminable loss. A lifetime of pain and guilt when the people he'd loved were taken. He wouldn't go near it again. He *couldn't* go near it again.

But God help him, he wanted things today he'd never imagined he'd ever want. *Ever.* It was the way she'd come apart for him earlier, so soft and hot beneath him. It was the way she'd watched him in the chapel, her eyes solemn on his.

It was the simple, searing fact that no one had ever had her but him. No one had ever touched her and therefore nobody truly knew her, except him. Cairo didn't need to be told that she'd given him a gift far more precious than her maidenhead today.

He'd spent his whole life doing what he had to do, not what he wanted to do. He always made the smart choice no matter how it hurt him, no matter what it cost. He'd learned long ago to think of himself and his own feelings last, if ever, because what the hell did *he* matter when there were so many lives on the line? He'd never questioned any of it. He'd become his own worst nightmare, an utter disgrace to all he held dear. And because of that, he'd survived.

He gazed down at the woman who fit as perfectly in his arms as he had inside her, and he didn't know if he could do it this time. For the first time in as long as he could remember, Cairo wanted to do more than simply survive.

He wanted *more.*

"You're staring at me." She sounded edgy, despite the smile she aimed at him. Because, of course, they were still in public. They were always in public.

"You are my wife." He sounded like the man he'd taken such care, all his life, to keep from becoming in word or deed or public perception. He sounded like his memories of his father, commanding and sure. His father, who had refused to fight the coup because he'd thought that meant fewer of his subjects would die. His father, who had always viewed his exile as a mere interlude. His father, the king of Santa Domini Cairo would never, ever become. "My queen."

Her dark eyes glittered despite the sunlight, and she seemed as far away then as if she was up on the stage in that club again. On display to all, available to none.

But he'd seen beneath that mask. He'd removed his own.

Everything was different now.

He didn't want to watch her distance herself from him or what had already happened between them today.

He wanted anything but distance, even when they were out in public for all to see.

He dipped her then, slow and romantic and not entirely for show, and let himself enjoy the way her gaze spit fire at him despite the smile she kept welded to her lips. He pressed a kiss against that smile when he pulled her back to standing, and let that kick between them.

That lick of fire. That spiked edge of need.

And the murmurs and applause from the crowd he'd half forgotten all around them.

"That felt like a threat," she told him through her teeth, her smile as bright as her clever eyes were dark, making her even more beautiful to him, somehow.

"It was a promise," he retorted.

Searing and hot, that promise.

One he had every intention of keeping.

And keeping and keeping, until he wore them both out.

Soon.

Brittany woke up sprawled across the wide bed in one of the private jet's guest chambers. She was still wearing the pale yellow shift dress that had been set out for her to change into after the wedding breakfast, and in which she'd been photographed by a sea of paparazzi as she and Cairo had boarded his plane in Italy the night of their wedding.

She'd staggered on board, put as much distance as possible between her and the brand-new husband who'd gotten under her skin in more ways than she could possibly count already, and then slept like the dead the moment she'd tossed herself across the soft coverlet.

She was all too aware he'd let her go. Let her retreat from him.

And now you're waking up married, she told herself—perhaps a little more sharply than she should.

After all, it wasn't as if that was anything new.

The fact that she was no longer a virgin, on the other hand, was.

Lying there on her stomach, she pulled her hand out from beneath the pillow and stared at her rings. She'd worn wedding sets before, of course. Her first husband had been as deficient in that department as in everything else, but Carlos had dutifully presented her with not only the expected solitaire engagement ring and a platinum band to match, but also a bill for her half of the investment they were making in their Hollywood future. Jean Pierre had preferred yellow gold and had given her an ornate ruby he'd claimed was a family heirloom when they'd gotten engaged, then two guard bands of rubies and diamonds at their wedding ceremony. His fifty-year-old matron of a daughter had sneered at the rings and told Brittany it looked like her hand had been dipped in blood.

"Success," Jean Pierre had murmured into Brittany's ear, the conniving old fool.

But today she wore the Heart of Santa Domini and next to it, an eternity band of heart-stoppingly perfect diamonds that sparkled with their own, deep fire.

Because this time she was married to a legend. She was Cairo Santa Domini's queen. Whatever happened next, however their fake little marriage worked and then ended, she would always—*always*—be the first woman he'd married. She would appear in all his biographical information, in history books and encyclopedias alike.

Just as he would always be the first—something inside her whispered *only*, but she shoved it aside as so much damaging wishful thinking—lover she'd ever taken.

Brittany rolled over and sat up, looking around the compact room as if she expected to see her new husband lurking somewhere. As if Cairo was the sort who lurked. But she was alone. The little room was dark. She had no idea what time it was, how long she'd slept, or even where they were flying. Cairo had announced that they would honeymoon for a month or two and that had been all the information he'd offered. She hadn't asked where they were headed because it hadn't much mattered. The Maldives, New York City, the moon—who cared?

Their act was their act wherever they took it.

She scraped her hair back into a knot at the nape of her neck, wishing she'd had time to comb it all out and shower after the wedding. Wishing she hadn't slept in all her makeup, come to that. She ran her index fingers below her eyes and sighed when they came away smudged with black mascara. *How regal and queenly*, she chided herself. No wonder Cairo had married her for the sole purpose of parading her embarrassing low-class behavior in front of the whole world. She couldn't even manage to wash her own face.

None of this felt real to her, the fact she'd married the most famous exile alive, and not just because she didn't like thinking about *why* Cairo had married her.

Her other marriages had felt real. Too real, in all the wrong ways. Her first wedding night had been spent locked in the bathroom of the run-down motel Darryl had taken her to before he'd started drinking himself into a rage. She'd been so naive then, thinking *drunk* was the worst thing a man could be. Darryl had quickly taught her otherwise. Her marriage to Carlos had been pure business all the way through, and their life together had been entirely conducted to be filmed, from their choice of apartment in the gritty outskirts of Los Angeles's Echo Park neighborhood, a far cry from the Hollywood tourists loved, to their plotted outings to Southern California hot spots. Even her time with Jean Pierre, which had been all about creating a commotion, had been conducted as a shared vision and business enterprise.

Her new marriage didn't feel particularly authentic in that sense. She certainly didn't feel like any kind of queen, exiled or otherwise. But *she* felt something far more than real. Cairo knew her deepest, darkest, best-kept secret.

She felt raw all the way through.

Brittany moved to the edge of the bed and helped herself to the bottle of spring water that had been left there, gulping down half of it in greedy swallows, but she still felt parched.

You are going to remember this moment with every step you take down that aisle, he'd promised her, and he'd been right. She'd felt soft and shivery all the way through the ceremony. She'd *felt* the vows he'd made as if he was still moving deep and wild between her legs, and she'd hardly managed to get her own out in turn.

There were a thousand things she should have been thinking about now that she was awake. She knew that. That they hadn't used any protection, for one thing. But she couldn't worry about that. Not now. Her mind skidded away from that and she found all she really wanted to know was where her brand-new husband was and why he wasn't in this bed with her, teaching her more of all the many marvelous things he knew.

She wanted to learn each and every one of them, and she didn't care how vulnerable it might make her feel. Or she'd care later, she told herself firmly. After he was gone and she had the rest of her life to live without him.

Not that she wanted to think about that inevitability. It would come soon enough. And in the meantime, she could indulge the sensual side of herself she hadn't known she possessed. Until Cairo.

Brittany heard a muffled buzzing sound then and it took her a long moment to realize it was her mobile phone. She looked around the room, finally spotting her handbag on the floor near the foot of the bed, where she must have dropped it in her earlier exhausted haze. She moved to yank the bag up from the floor, thinking as she did that the fact it was buzzing at all meant they had to be above land somewhere, not an ocean, or there wouldn't have been a signal.

Brittany glanced at the display, saw it was her mother and then answered the call anyway.

A choice she regretted almost instantly.

"Well, well," Wanda Mae Hollis said in her gravelly smoker's voice, thick with its usual resentment. "How nice of your uppity majesty to pick up the phone. I've been calling you for weeks."

"Hi, Mama," Brittany said, and it was harder than it should have been to mask her emotions. It annoyed her that there were any to mask. Phone calls from her mother were always assaults of one sort or another. She should have been used to it by now—and she was. That was why she usually avoided them. "I've been a little bit busy."

She sounded more Mississippi when she spoke to her mother than she did at any other time, ever. Her voice flattened out into the drawl she'd worked so hard to leave behind her when she'd left home, as if she was still that miserable child trying to make herself small in the corner of her mother's trailer while another drunken adult fight raged on.

"You don't need to tell me what you've been up to," Wanda Mae said bitterly. "It's all anyone can talk about today, no matter where we go. I hope you're happy with yourself."

This was why Brittany limited phone conversations. She didn't know why she'd answered this one. Did she want to punish herself? But she suspected she knew what it was that had made her pick up the call: that tiny little shred of hope she kept tucked away, deep inside of her, and only took out from time to time when it whispered things like, "maybe your mother might be happy for you for once."

That little shred was always wrong. Hope, she'd discovered long ago, was a big fat liar.

Brittany snuck an arm around her own waist and held on tight, then dug her bare toes into the carpeted floor beneath her as if she needed to remember that she was solid. That she was real. That she had a whole life that had nothing to do with Wanda Mae Hollis, and nothing her mother said could matter one way or the other unless she let it.

But she still didn't hang up. She didn't know why.

"Thank you," she said instead, and made an effort to sound as if she'd never visited Mississippi, much less grown up there. "I appreciate you calling with your good wishes."

Wanda Mae snorted. "I couldn't walk three feet today without someone else throwing your latest exploits in my face. Do you know what they're saying about you? Do you care?"

"I'll assume they're not praising me and calling me the next Kate Middleton," Brittany said, and was proud of the fact she sounded amused. Or close enough to amused, anyway, that the mother who barely knew her wouldn't be able to tell the difference. "But that's just a guess."

"Trust you to marry a king and screw that up, too," Wanda Mae snapped.

Brittany sighed. "I did it to hurt you, of course. You've discovered the truth."

"You think you're so smart, don't you?"

Her mother didn't wait for an answer. She kept right on talking, the way she always did.

The sick part, Brittany understood then as she listened to the usual litany of complaints and accusations that followed after that rhetorical question, was that she found this comforting on some level. She clenched her free hand into a fist and felt her rings dig into her flesh, but still, this was some kind of cold, bracing comfort. It reminded Brittany who she was and, worse, who she might have become.

Nothing had ever made Wanda Mae treat her eldest

child as anything but an embarrassing burden, no matter how much money Brittany had sent home over the years, which was never, ever enough. Nothing had ever made Wanda Mae act as if she loved Brittany at all, for that matter. Not Grandmama. Not her other kids, most of whom Brittany had basically raised herself while Wanda Mae was out cavorting in bars. Not the fact Brittany was the only one who hadn't gotten in any trouble. She hadn't gotten pregnant and she hadn't gone to jail. She'd just left.

And still, somehow, Brittany found her mother's predictable fury soothing. She knew what to expect, and no matter that it was the same endless font of vitriol every time. It was her mama. It was the way things had always been. *You probably need to take a look at that*, she told herself, not for the first time.

After all, she'd lost her virginity at last. She'd never thought that would happen. Didn't that suggest anything could?

But not today. Not when she felt so…ripped up inside. It was as if those stolen, heated moments in the castle had done a whole lot more than throw her over a cliff she hadn't known existed. They had crumbled her foundations into dust.

Cairo had.

She didn't know what to do about it. She didn't know if anything could be done about it, come to that. And her mother was still shooting off her mouth, the way she liked to do when she got going.

No wonder she'd answered this call. Somewhere deep inside, Brittany had obviously wanted to know that something, somewhere, would remain the same no matter how much she might have changed. No matter how much Cairo had already changed her, from the inside out, leaving her flailing about without a mask when she needed one the most.

"Only you could manage to marry the one person on earth more sinful and shameful than you are," Wanda Mae was saying as if personally affronted by this. "How am I supposed to hold my head up in town, Brittany?"

"I've never known how to answer that question, Mama," she replied, unable to keep the weariness from her voice. "But I'd imagine you should use your neck, like anyone else."

"I'm glad you can still make smart remarks. I'm glad you think this is one more big joke, like everything else in your life. Everyone knows exactly what kind of sick pervert that man is. Everyone knows what he's like. It's probably why you chose him. You *like* degenerate, disgusting—"

Brittany didn't know she meant to move and she had no memory of doing it, but then she was standing there by the side of the bed as if she'd *jumped* up. Her heart pounded at her, suggesting she had.

"Careful, Mama," she said, and her voice was cold. A kind of blade, slicing through her mother's stream of words and shocking them both, if her mother's gasp was any indication. "Be very careful. Keep running your mouth about him and you might find the bank dries right up. Then how will you keep yourself in cigarettes and beer?"

"You would threaten your own mother?"

"I don't want to hear your thoughts on this marriage."

Wanda Mae sniffed. "This is the influence that man has on you. This is the kind of ungrateful, selfish creature you've turned into, in such company. Flaunting yourself all over the world and then taking it out on your poor—"

"This is your last warning," Brittany said, even colder. "I'm not playing with you, Mama. He is off-limits to you."

Her mother fell quiet, and Brittany couldn't seem to feel that shocking little victory the way she should. She felt too unsteady. Her stomach was twisted into a knot and her heart was pounding at her. And she couldn't remember the last time she'd defended her choices to her mother. Had she ever?

But she refused to listen to her mother vent her spleen on Cairo.

She refused.

She didn't really want to ask herself why.

"You listen to me, Brittany," her mother said after a long pause, and her voice had gone quiet. Brittany closed her eyes and braced herself. "You think I don't know anything. You lit out of Gulfport and never looked back and believe you me, your opinion of the folks you left behind couldn't be more clear. You think we're all dumb country trash."

"I think nothing of the kind," Brittany gritted out, and what she hated herself for the most was how guilty she felt when her mother said these things. As if Brittany's snobbery had been the problem instead of Wanda Mae's patented blend of neglect and malice. "I think you'd find just as much about me to criticize if I lived next door."

"But I know a few things about rich men and poor girls," Wanda Mae continued as if Brittany hadn't said a word. "There's nothing new about it."

"Haven't you heard, Mama? I'm not all that poor any longer. If I was, you wouldn't get all those checks."

"This is one of the oldest, saddest, most run-of-the-mill stories around." Her mother's voice was upsettingly even. Not harsh. Not cruel. As if she was relaying a simple fact, nothing more. "Rich men like to play their games. They like to put a pretty girl on their arm and make a show out of it. They like to make sure everyone knows what a sacrifice they're making, taking on a charity project like her, so young and so desperate. And then they make those girls pay for the privilege. They make them pay and pay and pay. You might end up with more money, but you better believe that man will take whatever's left of your soul."

Brittany opened her mouth to say "you don't know him," but stopped herself just in time, horrified.

As if she did? As if anyone did? He'd been *inside her body* and she didn't know him at all.

"Thank you, Mama," she forced herself to say through lips gone stiff. "I'll keep that in mind."

She ended the call as her mother launched into another part of her lecture, then tossed the phone on the bed.

But she couldn't control the way she shook. The way her stomach flipped, end over end. Or the way her mother's words spun around and around in her head. As if Wanda Mae knew exactly how precarious this all was. As if she'd seen what Cairo had done to Brittany in that castle. How he'd touched her and, worse, how he'd made her feel.

What was going on with her that she'd tried to defend Cairo to her own mother when she hadn't defended *herself* in years?

"She's a lonely, bitter woman," Brittany told herself furiously, scowling at the mobile phone on the coverlet as if it was her mother's face, flushed with her usual anger. "You shouldn't listen to a word she says."

But her words disappeared the moment she said them, as if sucked out of the plane's windows and tossed off into the dark.

And her mother's words seemed to echo there instead, like a curse.

Like something worse.

Like prophecy.

CHAPTER EIGHT

THEY LANDED ON the small, private island in the Vanuatu archipelago as the South Pacific dawn eased its deep blue and fresh pink way across the sky.

"Vanuatu," Brittany murmured as they made their way down the jet's stairs to the private runway. She sounded shell-shocked. "You brought me to Vanuatu."

Cairo found he couldn't look away from her as she stopped at the bottom. There was the sea and the white sands and the sprawling house he'd bought on this faraway spot, but all he could see was his wife in a crumpled yellow dress and her hair in a tangled coil at her nape.

His wife, who he'd had to force himself not to pursue when she'd barricaded herself in that cabin for the whole of their twenty-hour flight. He'd reasoned she needed time. Space. Some peace and quiet after the circus that was their wedding. To come to terms with what had happened between them in that castle, perhaps—before they'd exchanged vows. To accept that they were truly married, in the classic sense of the term that involved the kind of consummation she'd never experienced before.

And if he allowed her space, he could pretend he hadn't needed it himself. That he wasn't shaken by what had happened. That it was nothing but sex, that moment she'd given herself to only him. That this marriage was yet one more circus sideshow, nothing more.

But she was his wife even so. The morning breeze from

the sea all around them was cool and soft, and teased the ends of the hair she'd braided to one side and tossed over her shoulder. She swallowed hard as she looked around, and he found himself watching the lovely line of her throat as if there were clues there. Answers to questions he didn't know how to ask.

"It looks exactly as I imagined it would," Brittany said quietly. Perhaps too quietly.

"Did you not wish to come here?" Cairo asked.

His own voice sounded unduly harsh in the quiet morning, with no other sounds but the surf and the breeze. He felt like a parody of himself. Even the clothes he wore seemed to brand him a fraud. A T-shirt that clung to his torso. Casual linen trousers. He felt like a beach bum instead of a king, or even the Euro-trash version of a king he'd been playing to the hilt all these years, and he found that made him…uneasy.

As if she would forget who he was if he gave her the chance. Or he would.

"I've always wanted to come here." She swallowed again, then blinked, as if she was shaking something off. Him? Their wedding? He didn't much care for that notion. "Eventually, I wanted to come here and stay forever."

"The island is yours," he said shortly. Gruffly.

Her gaze moved to his and he didn't like that it was troubled. He didn't like that at all.

"Mine? What do you mean, 'mine'?"

Cairo nodded to the waiting servants to handle their baggage and then took Brittany's arm, threading it through his. She didn't resist, and he found himself turning that over and over in his head like some hapless boy obsessing over his first sweetheart. It appalled him. Deeply. He was frowning as they started up the winding path toward the house that waited at the widest part of the small island, all rolled-up walls and high ceilings to let the tropics inside. An island paradise, if he said so himself.

But all he could concentrate on was the feel of her skin against his. Her arm on his. The smallest, most innocuous touch he could imagine, and yet it pounded through him like fire.

He had never felt so naked in all his life.

"Consider this place a wedding gift." His voice was even rougher then.

Cairo didn't know what was wrong with him. He'd spent twenty hours sitting on a jet plane becoming more and more of a stranger to himself. As if he'd left every careful mask he'd ever worn behind at that castle in Italy. As if here, with this woman, he was a man. Not an exiled king. Not a disgrace.

He didn't have the slightest idea what that meant, only that it spun in him, making him feel something like drunk.

Brittany was frowning now. At him. "You can't hand out islands as presents. That's insane."

Cairo ignored that. He reveled in the simple feel of her arm against his. Her lithe body moving beside him as they walked through the gathering daylight. The silky tropical breeze that danced around them and over them, making him remember those moments he'd been deep inside her—

Remember them. Who was he kidding? He hadn't thought of anything else since it had happened. He hadn't really tried.

"I was beginning to think I'd married Sleeping Beauty." He thought he felt her stiffen slightly beside him, and he thought there must be something deeply wrong with him that he'd view that as a good thing. Or any other reaction she had, for that matter. As long as he got to her. "And here I am, a king without a country instead of the necessary Prince Charming. It would have been quite the PR disaster, don't you think?"

She glanced at him, then back toward the path that stretched ahead of them. "I was tired."

"Are you certain?"

"Am I certain I was tired?" She frowned at him then. "Yes. But if I'd been confused, the fact I've slept for hours and hours would have cleared it up for me."

"It was a twenty-hour flight, give or take."

"Then, yes, Cairo. I'd say I was tired."

He tried to smile. That same casual lazy smile he'd used all his life. It should have come easily to him, the way it always had, but his own mouth betrayed him. "Because I was starting to think you were hiding in that bedroom."

She didn't pull her arm from his and Cairo didn't know why that felt like a gift.

"Do I have a reason to hide from you?" she asked. Carefully.

He thought they were both a little too aware that she hadn't exactly denied it.

"You tell me."

But she didn't. They walked for a moment in silence. The waves surged against the shore and the palm trees clattered overhead. Her bright copper hair, thick and wild, unwound itself from her makeshift braid as it moved and flowed around her, and he knew how she tasted, now. He knew how soft and molten she was for him, and the noises she made when he moved deep inside her. He knew her.

Maybe that was why his heart kicked at him, making his whole chest hurt.

"I appreciate the thought," she said in what he thought was a remarkably stiff voice, here on a tropical island in the middle of a perfect blue sea in all directions. "But I can't accept an entire island. As a…bridal present for a wedding that has the shelf life of organic fruit."

A swift glance her way showed him nothing. Her expression was smooth. Composed. The way it always was, as if he'd never held the heat of her in his hand.

His chest hurt. Worse than before. He was fairly certain it was that temper of his he normally kept locked away. Or worse, the truth of himself he'd been hiding from all these years.

"I am afraid it is already done." He stopped moving when the path ended at the bottom of the sweeping lawn that led up to one of the house's many lanais. "The island is yours, as is everything on it. My attorneys transferred ownership the moment you said 'I do.'"

She managed to pull her arm from his without seeming to do it on purpose. Cairo might have admired the sheer efficiency of the gesture if he hadn't hated that he was no longer touching her.

"No."

Her voice was low. She crossed her arms and frowned out toward the horizon. And Cairo could have pretended he hadn't heard her. That she hadn't spoken.

He didn't know why he didn't.

"I apologize that the gift does not please you," he said stiffly. "Is it the size of the island? The house? Would you prefer something larger or more ornate? Dubai, perhaps?"

"Of course not." She shook her head, but she still didn't meet his gaze. "I grew up in a trailer with my mother, whatever boyfriend she had that week and four other kids. Any house containing a room I don't have to share is like heaven to me. This…" She jutted her chin toward the house and when she finally looked at him again, her eyes were much too dark. "The house is beautiful, Cairo. Everything here is beautiful. It's so much more than I imagined."

"Then I fail to see the problem."

He felt rooted to the ground. Frozen into place. Completely out of his element—and how could that be? How had this woman turned him so upside down? What the hell had she done to him?

But he thought he knew. He hadn't expected her to be a virgin. To be innocent. There was no place in his sad, soiled life for *innocence.* And because he hadn't been prepared, even after she'd given herself away and he'd guessed the truth, he'd simply…reacted. He hadn't planned out what he'd do. He hadn't performed his usual role.

Those moments with her on the bed in that castle were the most genuine he'd been in at least twenty years, and it was addictive. He wanted more. He wanted her. He wanted to be the man he was with her, not the role he played.

He wanted everything.

"This is the problem," Brittany said, and her tone was too even. "This is my dream. I told you that. *Mine.* You have no right to use it as part of this sick little farce we're acting out for the world's amusement."

"By which I am to assume you mean our marriage."

"Marriage, performance art—whatever you want to call it." She shrugged. "It's not real. Coming to Vanuatu is a dream that's sustained me for years. It's what I've held on to through every single horrible thing that's written about me or said to my face. It's what allows me to shrug it all off. How could you possibly imagine I'd want to pollute it with this thing? With—"

She cut herself off.

"Me?" Cairo supplied coolly, because she did not see a man. She saw the game. The roles he played. The creature he'd become.

"I don't know what you dream about," she threw at him, and his particular sickness was that he found that to be progress, that little show of temper. "I couldn't begin to guess."

"I am a king without a kingdom." Cairo laughed at that, though the sound was hollow, and he thought the breeze stole it away anyway. "What exactly do you imagine it is I dream about, Brittany?"

"I dream about something that's mine," she snapped at him, and he saw the way she gripped herself tighter, as if she was holding herself back. Or holding herself together. "All mine. Where no one is watching me and speculating about me and making up stories about me. I dream about a perfect, unspoiled place a million miles away from the rest of the world, where I can disappear. Do you have the slightest notion what that means?"

"I'd imagine it means a well-staffed house accessible only by boat or by air, in the farthest reaches of one of the most remote island nations on earth." He eyed her, standing there with her feet in the sand and the South Pacific around her because he'd imported her straight into her fantasy. "Wherever will we find such a place, do you think?"

"I play a part, Cairo. A role." Her words came fast and hard now, and he found he enjoyed watching her unravel far more than he should. It meant this was getting to her, too. That he was. Cairo couldn't regret that. "I've been playing it since I was a kid. Vanuatu was supposed to happen when I finally left it all behind, not while I'm neck-deep in the middle of yet another performance!"

Something eased inside him then, though that pressure in his chest remained. He thought the way she scowled at him was beautiful. He thought *she* was beautiful—even more so than the island paradise that waited all around them.

He saw the way her lips trembled slightly before she pressed them together. He saw the way she leaned back, as if she'd wanted to put more space between them, but had forced herself to stand still.

This wasn't affecting only him. He wasn't the only one without a mask.

"Come here," he said. It was more of an order.

Cairo had the distinct pleasure of seeing that melting expression move over her face before she balked, visibly, and straightened where she stood. He *felt* it, everywhere. In that pressing thing in his chest. In his sex.

"I'm standing one foot away from you," she said, crossly, and he was insane to find that tone of voice comforting. He was a madman, there was no other explanation.

But he didn't care.

He sighed in the officious manner that had servants at aristocratic balls leaping to tend to his every whim, and then he merely reached across that one foot of space, hooked his hand around her neck and hauled her to him.

She hit his chest an instant later, made one of those soft noises that made the hunger in him burn white-hot and threw her head back to look up at him. She was scowling, of course. She was always scowling. But that meant she wasn't hiding behind her mask of composure, and Cairo loved it. He craved it. He wanted more.

"Cairo—"

"This is not a performance," he told her, holding her where he wanted her, her body flush against his. *Where she belongs*, something in him whispered. "You, me. Here. None of this is for public consumption. It is only ours. It is real."

The truth was the way she flushed at that. The way her eyes darkened with the same need he felt careening around inside of him, changing him. Changing the whole world.

"There's no such thing as *ours*," she whispered. "There's nothing *real* here."

"Tesorina," he murmured, "of course there is. It tastes like this."

And then he bent his head to claim her mouth, and showed her exactly what he meant.

* * *

The weeks that followed were like a dream. The best version of her favorite dream, in fact.

Brittany never, ever wanted to wake up.

It wasn't only that the house and island were even more beautiful than she could have imagined they'd be. It wasn't that they were staffed to the extraordinary level of discreet, nearly psychic level of service that Cairo demanded. That meant that almost the moment they had a thought or a desire, often before it was expressed, the plate of food was laid out or the tray of drinks was presented. That meant fresh towels and a selection of new, tropical clothing to better while away the days every time they exited one of the property's pools, or wandered out of the sauna. That meant the tiki torches were always lit the instant the sky began to turn colors at the end of the day and there was always a hammock waiting between two palm trees should they take a walk along the beach.

All of that was divine. Luxurious pampering far beyond anything Brittany had ever imagined. But far more remarkable than the level of service was the solitude. Their first night there, after Cairo had carried Brittany off to the vast master suite they'd shared ever since and after they'd worked off their jet lag in the most delectable manner possible, they'd agreed to simply…shut out the world.

"No one will miss us for five weeks," Cairo had said when evening had started to creep across the sky, orange and red, outside the open floor-to-ceiling spaces where walls would be in another house. "They will barely notice we are gone, with so many other headlines to keep them occupied."

He'd been sprawled out on his back on the bed, the sheets in complicated tangles at his feet. Brittany had been stretched out over him, the dizzying heat they'd built in each other still there where she pressed against him, even as the lazy ceiling fan moved the cooler air around on her back. Her head had been a cascade of images of all the ways they'd had each other already in that single, perfect, endless day. All the things he could do with his hands, his mouth. All the places on that stunning body of his she'd tested with hers.

Her body had still been humming. She thought perhaps it always would.

"I suppose we have the rest of our lives to be terrible," she'd agreed drowsily, unable to think of much beyond the simple perfection of the way their bodies fit together. The way they seemed perfectly crafted to come together like this and drive each other wild—

There had been something in her that had balked at that, deep down beneath the layers of satisfaction. She might not have had sex with anyone before Cairo, but she wasn't a complete idiot. She knew sex made people crazy. It made them imagine intimacies that didn't exist outside the bed. Hadn't she watched her own mother make that mistake again and again? Brittany had always vowed she'd never be one of those deluded fools, no matter what.

But she could put that aside for a little over a month, too, she'd thought then. She could simply sink into this thing and not worry about what came after or how she'd have to play it when they went back to their carefully scripted, relentlessly public lives. She could decide not to worry about it—about anything that wasn't Cairo, or herself, or how they made each other feel—until this honeymoon was over. And until then, they could lock their phones and laptops in one of the cupboards and let themselves soak in the peace and quiet of this little island so far away from anything.

"I think this is the purpose of a honeymoon," she said.

Cairo smiled, his hand moving lazily down the length of her spine, then back up again. "I thought it was an opportunity to post pictures from exotic locales onto one's social media pages, the better to maintain one's presence and public brand. No? Are you sure?"

"Ask me in a month," Brittany replied, grinning as she buried her face in that tempting hollow between his pectoral muscles.

Their days bled one into another, long and sweet. They walked on the beaches in the sun and in the intermittent rains that kept the plants lush. They sat beneath the impossible confusion of stars at night, out on one of the terraces or huddled together on a blanket on the sand. They talked, ate, swam. They argued politics and classic movies. They read books from the house's eclectically stocked libraries, discussed them, then read more.

And they explored each other, with a ferocity and focus that would have shaken Brittany to her core if she'd stopped to think about it. She didn't. It seemed part and parcel of these stolen blue-sky weeks. It seemed as inevitable as the afternoon rains, the kick of the tropical winds, the smudged blue line of the horizon far away in the distance. She abandoned herself to Cairo's touch the same way she lost herself in a novel or sank beneath the sea to listen for whale songs. No thought, no concern, no self-preservation.

There were no kings on this island, no class divisions, no strippers and no scandal. There was only the glory of the way her body took him in, again and again. There was only the sweetness of the way they came together in the lazy heat, the bold explosions of need and hunger they weathered in the pool, on the beach, standing near the trees, down on the floor of the room they liked to read in.

Brittany had never known another person's body as well as she came to know Cairo's. Every inch of his skin. Every tiny imperfection that made his intense male beauty that much more fascinating to her. She tasted her way across the acres of his sculpted chest and lost herself in the taut ridges of his abdomen. She licked him where he was salty and slept tangled up with him in that great big bed. She learned how to straddle him and take him into her, how to ride them both blind, and how to tease him with the slow, careful rhythm of her hips until he could only groan. She learned how to love him with her mouth, sucking him and licking him until he sank his fingers in her hair and bucked against her, emptying himself between her lips.

And she had never been known so comprehensively in return.

Oh, the things Cairo taught her about herself. About her appetites and her capacity for both pleasure and need. There was no boundary he wouldn't cross, no limit he wouldn't push, if he thought it would make her scream.

It usually did.

He was insatiable. She lost count of the times he reached for her at night, or the times their gazes snagged during the day and led to more of that bone-melting fire they fanned high in each other again and again.

It couldn't last. She told herself that *of course* it couldn't last, but perhaps that was what made it so poignant.

Or that was what Brittany told herself as the weeks rolled by, slow and bright and more beautiful than anything she'd ever dared imagine. Better than she ever could have dreamed that night she'd rejected his initial proposal in Monte Carlo. Just…*better.*

Because the other thing they did with all their time together was talk. Rambling conversations that started one day and ended the next, and that Brittany only realized later were deeply revealing. Stories comparing their very different childhoods, painted in broad strokes and told as if they'd been amusing, when they weren't. Current events, popular culture in at least three countries, even the odd conversation about sports—all these things, taken together, meant not only that she knew the exiled king of Santa Domini better than anyone alive, but that he also knew her the same way.

Inside and out, that little voice inside her reminded her daily. *No masks. No act. Just you.*

She told herself it didn't scare her, such astonishing intimacy. Because she wouldn't let it.

One night, after they'd had their usual dinner of fresh grilled seafood and an array of perfect fruits, they sat out on one of the terraces beneath the night sky. The flames on the tiki torches danced in the faint breeze from the water, and they were tucked up together on one of the loungers. Brittany sat between Cairo's legs, her back to his chest, and absently ran her fingers through his.

It had been a month, and the fact of that had been echoing inside her all day. It reminded her that this wasn't forever. That this relaxed, smiling man who was all caramel and whiskey when he looked at her here would disappear, and soon. They would put on more clothes and walk back onto the stage where they conducted their lives and had already made plans to end their brand-new marriage, and these weeks would be the anomaly.

She would have to wake up, and she didn't want that. More to the point, she would have to deal with the growing worry deep inside of her that the fact she'd missed her period for the first time in her life, two weeks into their stay, was from something more than the stress of such a major life change.

Brittany didn't want to consider that, much less what it might mean if her suspicions were correct. All the things it might mean, when their relationship had a built-in expiration date. A child was forever, no matter their messy divorce.

A child would change everything.

"You seem far away."

Cairo's voice was rich and lazy, but Brittany knew that, here, it was because he was actually relaxed. She couldn't bring herself to ruin that. She felt the words on her tongue and swallowed them back.

They had so little time left before they were back in the world. It could wait.

"We only have a week left here." She blew out a breath and told herself it was kinder to wait until she knew for certain. Better. "It's going to be hard to leave. To get back onstage and into the headlines."

Her hair curled as it pleased in the humidity here, and after the first day or two of fighting it she'd simply let it do what it would. Behind her, Cairo wrapped a long curl he found around his finger, winding it tighter and tighter, then let it loose only to start all over again.

"What would you do?" he asked idly. Or perhaps not idly at all. "If there were no headlines. If there was only a normal life to live."

"A normal good life or a normal bad life?" she asked, tipping her head back to better rest against his shoulder.

His mouth, still the most gorgeous thing imaginable, grazed her forehead in a glancing kiss that still managed to make that glowing heat deep inside her spike.

"I believe that is the trial of normal life, is it not? One cannot tell, day to day. One is without the constant intervention of the press, there to interpret every move and fashion it into a narrative that sells papers. If that is good or bad is up to you."

"I want picket fences," Brittany said, surprising herself. But once she said it, she warmed to the idea. "I want to cook things, feed a family, worry about the school run and the ladies at the PTA. I want the life they live in minivan commercials, with golden retrievers and a good soundtrack."

She felt his laughter, deep in his chest.

"You would not get to dance in that life. The picket fences forbid it, I think."

She smiled at that. "I'd dance for fun, not money. That's the problem with being good at what you love. You turn it into your job and then it can't be about love anymore. It has to be about bills." She laughed. "Not that you'd know much about bills, I think."

"I pay my bills." Cairo's voice was ripe with the same laughter she'd felt in his chest, and that wealth of affection that she knew would fade, out there. Out in all those spotlights and flashbulbs. And it would likely happen very quickly if she really was pregnant. She shoved that aside. "Larger ones, I imagine, than most."

He pulled her closer to him. She could feel the heat of him through the gauzy layer of the flowing dress she wore. The heat and the steel-edged strength that was all Cairo. With his arms around her and his body surrounding her, Brittany felt hollowed-out and whole at once.

"What would you do?" she asked. "If you could choose a normal life, what would it be?"

He was quiet for a long time. Brittany could feel the solid weight of him behind her and feel the soothing beat of his heart against her back. She listened to the waves in the distance as she waited, and tried to tip herself over and out into the stars spread out so thickly above them.

"I do not think I know what normal is," Cairo said, when she'd stopped expecting that he might respond. He sounded quieter than before. "I do not know what it looks like."

"You could be an accountant," she said, crinkling up her nose at the image of his highness, the imperious accountant. "Or, I know, a traveling bard. Can you sing? That would work better if you sang, of course."

"The only thing I know how to be is me," Cairo said, and there was a strange note in his voice then.

Brittany didn't think. She shifted around on the lounger, moving so she could straddle him and loop her arms around his neck. She looked down into his perfect face. Those impossible cheekbones, that purely Santa Domini jaw he deliberately left unshaven, as if that could obscure the truth of him. As if anything could, exile or a thousand mocking headlines or his own penchant for self-destruction.

She felt him stir beneath her, and felt her own body, so attuned to him now, instantly ready itself for his possession. But she made no move to impale herself on him, to throw them both back into that slick, breathless heat. She only searched his royal face in the starlight, and that odd expression in his dark amber eyes.

"Then that's normal," she said. "That's your normal life. Why should you change?"

Cairo's mouth curved. "I like it when you are fierce on my behalf, *tesorina.* The truth is I have never adapted." He shrugged, and she expected him to kiss her. To change the subject with his touch as he usually did. She was shocked when he kept speaking. "I was bred to be the king of Santa Domini. My father might have been exiled, but he always imagined that was a temporary state of affairs. He had every intention of reclaiming his throne." His jaw hardened, and though his hands were at her hips she could see his attention was far in the past. "Even after he died, nothing changed. I was the unofficial king. I was always me. It didn't matter how many ways I made it clear I was unfit to rule. Every person I trusted expected that someday, I would take back the kingdom. All these years later, they still do." His gaze found hers, hard and stirring and filled with a darkness that tugged at her. "What is normal for me, Brittany, is to be the greatest disappointment my people have ever known."

"No." The word was out before she knew she meant

to speak, but she didn't stop. She continued, feeling very nearly furious—but *for* him, not *at* him. "Nothing about you is disappointing."

Something sparked in his gaze then. He lifted a hand to slide it over her cheek, anchoring his fingers in her hair as if he'd hold her there forever. As if he could.

"You cannot be trusted," he told her softly. "You make me imagine I could be not only a decent man, but the man I was intended to become. You are so far under my spell you cannot see straight."

"You're wrong, Your Majesty," she whispered back, still fierce and sure, and finally using the title that he deserved. *His* title. "You're pure magic."

The way he looked at her then, so certain that that was the sex talking and it could never, ever be true, broke her heart.

And that was when she knew. It wasn't a jolt or a shock. It was as inevitable as the next wave against the gleaming white sand. The sun sinking into the sea. It washed through her, changing her completely from one moment to the next, though nothing had changed. She loved him. She wondered if she always had, even back in that first moment when she'd seen him across a casino floor and had been struck dumb. She'd known this would happen from the start.

This was the ruin, the destruction, she'd feared all along. *Love.* As simple and as terrifying as that.

She'd spent a month here with absolutely no mask. She'd given him her virginity. She'd opened herself up to him in a thousand ways she hadn't known were possible, and she thought that no matter what happened next, even if she really was pregnant, she couldn't regret it. She wouldn't.

But she couldn't tell him, either.

Because she knew without having to ask that love was

the one thing that could ruin everything between them. Worse, perhaps, than the possibility of a child.

"No, *tesorina*," Cairo said, that look in his eyes that made her heart feel shattered. Sad and wise and lost, as if they were already back in Europe. As if she'd already had to give him up, the way they'd planned. As if he'd known all along that this dream of theirs could never last. She'd known that, too. And it hadn't done a single thing to stop this. Any of this. "You are the magic."

And then he pulled her mouth to his.

She kissed him back, a sharp desperation snaking through her. Because every kiss was measured now. Every touch was closer to their last.

She wriggled against him, lifting herself up so she could find him in his linen trousers and free the satin length of him between them. The fire that always raged in them both was a madness tonight, the flames wild and almost harsh, and Brittany shook as she waited for him to handle their protection, as he'd done every single time save their first. She let out a soft sound of distress when he pulled his mouth from hers, and he didn't laugh at her the way he usually did.

Neither one of them was in a playful mood.

She felt the blunt head of his sex against her softness, and she rolled her hips to take him inside of her. She worked herself down, rocking gently until she was seated fully against him.

Cairo let out a long, hard breath. Brittany wrapped her arms around his shoulders and then, giving in to an urge she didn't want to name, tipped her forehead to his. For an eternity, they sat there like that, drinking each other in. Her husband. Her king. Possibly the father of her child. For as long as she had him.

He was huge and hard within her, she was soft and trembling. Their mouths were so close she could breathe with him if she liked, and it was as if they'd both realized how close they were to losing this. How very short, indeed, the week they had remaining to them was.

She started to move then, and this time, it was a dance. It was joy.

It was love.

Brittany couldn't say it, she didn't dare say such a thing to the man she'd married purely for the headlines, so she showed him. Every roll of her hips, every lift and every slide. He peeled the straps of her dress down and took one of her hard nipples into his mouth, driving her wild as she loved him with every last part of her being. He pulled hard and she let her head drop back, and then it really was as if she'd fallen off into all those stars.

It was hard to tell who did what. There was only sensation and fire, bliss and longing.

Love, she thought, with each delirious thrust, but then she stopped thinking altogether.

And there was only Cairo.

He reached down between them and pressed hard where she needed him most, and Brittany exploded—but he didn't stop. He surged into her, pounding her straight through one exultant climax and high again toward another.

He flipped them over on the lounger, coming over her in the soft, silken night as he thrust himself home.

Deeper. Harder. Better than perfect.

Again and again and again.

Until they flew over that edge together.

And stayed there beneath the quiet glory of the southern stars until the first hint of a brand-new morning, when everything changed.

CHAPTER NINE

RICARDO ARRIVED ON the island via very noisy helicopter from Port Vila, Vanuatu's capital city, not long after the break of dawn.

He was not welcome, Cairo thought uncharitably as he watched his most loyal subject walk toward him over the otherwise deserted beach, the crisp suit he wore that was so appropriate in Paris looking nothing but out of place here.

It was a stark reminder of how far away Cairo had been from the world this last month—and how much he'd like to remain here forever.

"Was I expecting you?" Cairo asked. He led Ricardo onto the lanai where breakfast was usually served, and nodded toward the carafe of strong, hot coffee he knew the man preferred. "I feel certain I was not."

It was more of an effort than it should have been to keep his tone light. Lazy and careless, as expected. He'd grown unused to speaking to anyone but Brittany—and he'd thought he'd be able to keep it that way a while longer.

The truth was, he didn't *want* to speak to anyone but Brittany. He hadn't wanted to leave her when the sound of the helicopter had woken them both where they'd drowsed off together beneath the light blanket he'd pulled over them sometime in the middle of the night. He'd had to let her go, and he didn't like that edgy, pointed sort of feeling that had moved into his chest lately, to go along with that pressure that never really eased.

He didn't like any of this.

"You have been out of reach for a month, Sire," Ricardo replied, pressing a mug of coffee to his lips. He took a pull, relaxed his shoulders, then focused on Cairo again. "Completely out of reach. There were rumors that you were dead."

Cairo waved a hand. "There are always rumors."

"These were more convincing, given the absence of the usual photographic evidence to the contrary."

"I would never die in so obscure a fashion," Cairo murmured, and some part of him was dismayed at how easy it was to pick up his role again. To slip back into that second skin of his and treat it like it was the only one he knew. "Especially not so tragically young. I would make certain to die theatrically in a major city, the better to leverage good media coverage of my pageant of a funeral."

"Sire." Ricardo's expression was…not grim, exactly. *Solemn*, Cairo thought. And something rather more like *expectant*. "General Estes suffered a massive heart attack a few days ago. He collapsed in the palace and was rushed to the hospital, where, after many attempts to revive him, he died." He watched Cairo's face as if he expected a reaction. When Cairo only stared, he cleared his throat. "His ministers have stepped in and are trying to maintain the peace, but they have never been anything but puppets. You know this. And, Sire. The people…" Ricardo made no attempt to hide the gleam in his gaze when he trained it on Cairo. The fervor, the belief. "Sire, the people are ready."

Time seemed to spread out. To flatten.

Cairo remembered his father's hand, heavy on his shoulder as they'd walked together through a foggy British morning on a remote estate, years ago now.

"What if we never go home?" Cairo had asked. He

could not have been more than eight years old. His father, then the exiled king to Cairo's crown prince, had seemed so old to him then. So wise and aged, when in truth he'd been an athletic man midway through his forties.

"It is your duty to carry Santa Domini within you wherever you go, whether we return home or not," his father had said. "You must serve the kingdom in all you do and say. All you are. Every step and every action, Cairo. That is your calling. Your destiny."

He'd never forgotten it. Not when they'd come to get him out of his history classroom that rainy winter day, bundling him off to a room where grim strangers frowned at him and pretended to be concerned for him. Not when they'd told him everyone he loved was dead and his world was forever altered. Not when he'd realized that he must be next on the general's assassination list, no matter that the man's involvement was never officially confirmed, and no matter how many people told him that it had been an accident.

Not when he'd wondered, in his grief, if he should let the general exterminate him, too. It would have been so much easier than fighting.

He'd thought of the kingdom then.

"There's only the prince now," the woman had said on the news. She'd been a village woman from one of the most remote spots in the kingdom. He'd watched her from a guarded hotel room somewhere outside of Boston, while the authorities investigated his family's death. He hadn't been permitted to attend their funerals, but he'd watched his people mourn. "He's all that we have left of our history."

He'd served the kingdom then, and lived. Santa Domini's history—but ever unfit to lead. He'd made sure of it.

He thought of the kingdom now.

He thought of the general, dead at last with all the

blood of Cairo's family still there on his hands. And the things that roared in him then had sharp claws. They left deep marks that he knew, from experience, would never go away.

He thought of the woman who had called him magic, who had seen him as no one else in all the world had ever seen him. And no one else ever would. He told himself he didn't understand what it was that tugged so hard and so insistently at his heart then, leaving him bleak.

He had made himself unfit to be a king. He could not undo that now. He could not erase the things he'd done, nor allow the man who'd done them—the man his father would have loathed—to sit upon that throne.

Cairo had no choice but to gaze back at Ricardo blandly.

"Ready for what?" he asked, and, oh, what it cost him to sound so bored. So disengaged. "The funeral? I'm sure the general's men will give him a good show." He paused, as if something occurred to him. "You must know *I* cannot set foot on Santa Dominian soil, Ricardo. Not even all these years later, when no one could possibly care either way."

He saw the incredulity on his man's face, followed by a flash of something as close to pure rage as he'd ever seen a servant show in his presence. And if that made him feel sick, if he loathed himself as much as his father might have had he lived to see what his son had become, that was neither here nor there.

This wasn't about him. It never had been.

"Ricardo," he said gently, "what game do you think we've been playing here? The goal is to remind the world at every turn that I am not fit to lead. Has that changed?"

"I thought..." Ricardo looked lost. "Sire, that was a game you played, but now it's ended. I assumed we were merely biding our time."

"You know what they say about making assumptions, I am certain."

Ricardo put his coffee down as if he feared he might otherwise drop it. Cairo opened his mouth to say something else, to hammer in the man's low impression of him even harder and deeper, but heard the faintest sound from behind him.

Cairo knew what he'd see before he turned to confirm it. He'd grown accustomed to the sound of that particular light step. Those particular bare feet against the stones. He'd know her anywhere.

Brittany stood there in the wide-open entry to the lanai, in the deep shadows of the house. She'd thrown on a different dress, this one a bright riot of colors that cascaded from a neat bow around her neck all the way to the ground. Her hair fell in the careless abandon he found endlessly compelling here, copper and bright, but her hazel eyes were too dark and fixed on him.

He'd kept telling himself that he was scratching an itch. Week after week after week. That one of these mornings he would wake up and find himself as bored with Brittany as he'd always been with every other woman alive. But an entire month had passed, and all he felt was this ceaseless *hunger*.

Cairo wanted to know what she thought. About the book she was reading, about the weather, about what she'd had for her breakfast, about the cloud formations stacked in the sky. He wanted to see what she would say next, on any topic. He loved the stories she'd tell about her Mississippi childhood, the drawl that slipped into her speech and the evident affection she had for the grandmother she'd lost when she was only nine.

He hated not touching her. He hated that she stood across the lanai from him and didn't come any closer, which felt like a slap after all these weeks. And he felt something very much like shame that she'd seen him transform, so easily and so heedlessly, from the man she'd woken up with into Cairo Santa Domini, professional joke.

"Did you hear?" he asked her, and he thought he was the only one who'd be able to see the way she reacted to that smug, bored voice he used like the weapon it was. The faint widening of her eyes. The quick breath she took, then held. "Ricardo has come all this way to update me on events that cannot concern me in the least."

"Sire," Ricardo tried again. "The ministers are the ones most interested in these rumors of your death. They want to move fast and elect another regent while pretending they think you've abdicated."

"Then I should stay where I am," Cairo said, sounding even more bored than before. "I cannot imagine anything less amusing than a riot. Let them work it out amongst themselves, without my involvement."

"Don't be silly." Brittany's voice was cool, composed. As sharp as it had been so long ago now, in Monte Carlo. It made him as hard as he'd been then. But this time, it came with a pervasive sense of sorrow at everything they'd lost when that helicopter landed. At all the things that must happen now. They'd agreed on it long before the general had died. "Of course, you must return to Europe."

"He needs to take his rightful place," Ricardo said, turning to Brittany as if he expected her to agree with him.

But her eyes met Cairo's from a distance that seemed much, much farther than merely across the lanai. And he thought he could feel that pressure in his chest cracking into pieces and shattering all around him, so loud and harsh he was surprised no one else seemed to hear it.

"I think my husband's rightful place is in the tabloids," she said, and it slid between his ribs like steel. Like a killing blow. Like love, he thought, vicious and deadly.

Because she knew him best, this woman. She knew him better than anyone, his destiny and his heart alike. She knew exactly how best to hurt him, and she did it. It made him wonder how he'd hurt her, to make her respond like this. But then it hardly mattered as she kept going. "The more lurid, the better. That is, after all, how we make our money."

Brittany waited for Cairo outside his expansive master suite in the historic Parisian residence. The one she didn't share. The one he'd told her was his before locating her and her things far away from him, down two floors and all the way in the other wing of the grand old house.

It had been a very long handful of days since they'd flown back from the island.

Paris had welcomed them with a glum drizzle and packs of paparazzi, and Brittany had felt…off. She'd assumed it was the culture shock. She'd assumed it was the difficulty in transitioning from a life lived in a sarong and a hammock to all the appearances at parties and balls and charity events that were expected of her, all to be recorded in snide detail in the papers.

She'd assumed it was that little secret deep inside her that she'd still been pretending might be something other than what she'd known, on a deep, feminine level, it was.

"I can't imagine they think you'll discuss the lines of ascension here," she'd said that first night as their car inched closer to the red carpet outside some or other film festival Cairo had insisted they attend. The cameras were everywhere. Squat, grizzled men had poured over the cars like ants, and waiting her turn to be picked apart was making Brittany feel anxious and faintly queasy. "I wish they'd leave us alone."

"You had better hope they do not," Cairo had replied from his side of the seat, where he kept his face buried in the paper. "As that would render you obsolete and wholly useless to me."

He'd been about that charming the entire way back from Vanuatu.

Two nights ago, he'd swept a cutting glance over her when she'd met him in the grand foyer of his museum of a residence.

"You look tired," he'd said flatly.

"How flattering." She'd hated that she had to work so hard to sound crisp and unbothered. That she couldn't switch back into her old role as easily as he had. "That was, of course, my goal for the evening."

He'd looked impatient. "There is no need to look so tragic. I am thinking only of the photographs." He frowned faintly as he took in her exquisite gown and the jewelry he'd picked out himself. "Perhaps that shade of red is not your color."

It had been the precise shade of red as the dress she'd worn at their engagement dinner.

"Cairo." She'd wished she hadn't bothered when he'd stared back at her as if he hardly recognized her. As if she was nothing to him. She'd felt like nothing, and later, she'd imagined, she would lie awake in her lonely bed where no one could see her and if she cried a little bit about that, nobody need know. "There is no need for you be *quite* so brusque. People might mistake you for a Royal Jackass."

She'd thought she'd seen the Cairo she knew in there. Just the faintest glimpse of him, behind all that dark amber. It had made her foolish.

"I know this isn't you," she'd said.

"Do you?" he'd asked icily, dangerously. "Because I find I have no idea what awaits me in that mirror every morning. I was meant to be a king, but I made myself a clown. A disgrace to my name. I have no earthly idea who I am—but you think you do?"

She'd shaken at that, but she'd met his tortured gaze. "I know you are a good man."

"You know nothing of the sort," he'd said coldly, furiously. "What you know is that I am good in bed, as I told you I was when we met. Do not paint me with all your feverish little fantasies, Brittany. I am not a good man. I have only ever been a monster, and it hardly matters why."

"Cairo—"

"You are no use to me run-down and dragging," he'd said then, cutting her off. "My suggestion to you is that you see a doctor and sort yourself out, or leave. Your choice."

The bastard.

She'd only realized she'd said that out loud when his mouth had curved in a far icier smile than the ones she'd known and basked in on their island. It made her heart ache inside her chest.

"I am afraid I am distressingly legitimate," he'd replied. As if it hurt him. His mouth had been grim, his caramel gaze dark. "Therein lies the problem."

Yesterday, she'd summoned Cairo's private physician. She'd paged through articles on her phone while the brisk woman bustled around her and gave her the news, and she'd tried to imagine what it must feel like for Cairo with the general finally dead and a kingdom he'd made certain he couldn't claim clamoring for his return. She'd told herself to be calm, to be understanding, and if all of that failed, to be quiet.

Because she'd known going into this that it would hurt. Why was she surprised that, sure enough, it did—if in a different way than she'd anticipated?

"What are you doing here, Brittany?"

She jerked back into the present to find herself on the little upholstered bench in the hall outside Cairo's bedroom. He stood a few feet away, dressed in one of his three-piece bespoke suits and his hair a calculated mess, his expression as distant as if they'd never met.

Brittany told herself she should hate him. But she didn't.

She didn't. She couldn't.

I have only ever been a monster, he'd said, and that made her want nothing more than to prove him wrong. It made her want to do all kinds of foolish things, like tell him she loved him.

She didn't dare.

"It's lovely to see you, too," she gritted out.

He managed to look as if he was sighing heavily while not actually moving, a skill she might have admired under different circumstances.

"We do not have an appointment," he told her. "If we did, it would not be in my bedroom. I will see you this evening as planned, for the—"

"Will we just pretend that it never happened?" she demanded, and she was horrified to hear her voice crack. But she pushed on. "That whole month was nothing more than a dream, is that it? Have you truly convinced yourself of that?"

"The honeymoon is over." His voice was like steel. "It never should have happened in the first place. This was always a business arrangement. We should have kept it on that level."

"It's a bit late for that," she said, and couldn't help the laugh that bubbled up then. "Much too late."

Another look of impatience flashed over his beautiful face, and he shook his head at her.

"Do you know who I am, Brittany? Have you met me? Read about me in any tabloid?"

She had an inkling of where he was going, of what he might say, and it felt like a car crash. As if she'd spun out of control already and there was nothing she could do to stop it—all the while perfectly cognizant of the tree she was seconds away from smashing against.

"What," Cairo asked, ruthless and cold, "ever gave you the impression that sex with you would distinguish you in any way from the thousands of women who came before you?"

Everything inside of Brittany went horribly still, then. Frozen solid.

It occurred to her that was a blessing.

She stood, carefully. She smoothed her hands over the sleek line of the dress she wore. She remembered herself, at last. It had been so hard to pull her public persona back onto her and wrap herself up in it again—but look at that. He'd just made it remarkably easy.

"Calm yourself," she told him, from miles away. Her voice was crisp and cold, and the great thing about the way he'd yanked her heart from her body and crushed it on the floor beneath his shoe was that it couldn't hurt her any longer. It was simply gone. "I wasn't forming the queue for a chance in your bed. Been there, done that, thank you."

His harsh expression didn't change.

"Then as I said, I will see you tonight. We have a very precise plan, Brittany. I suggest you stick to it."

"With pleasure," she replied. Then smiled pure ice at him. "One small wrinkle in the plan, however. I'm pregnant."

One sentence and the world crumbled. Cairo knew that better than most.

He'd never thought it would happen again. It had already happened twice. He'd never imagined he would once more find his world divided so tidily into *before* and *after.*

"How?"

That hardly sounded like him.

Brittany looked smooth and perfect, which he'd come to hate. She was so different here in Paris. So far from his island lover she might as well have been a different woman. Her hair was pulled back in a sleek chignon. She wore a tailored dress and her usual impeccable shoes. She looked like a glossy photograph of herself. She looked untouchable, and no matter if she was slightly pale.

She made him ache. She made him wish he was a different man—a better one.

Her expression turned faintly pitying.

"You're the one with battalions of experience, as you are so happy to share with me and every tabloid reporter in Europe. Surely you can figure out *how*."

Cairo could only stare at her, the world he knew falling apart in great chunks all around him, though the hall was quiet. Deceptively peaceful.

"You cannot be pregnant," he told her.

Another cool smile. "Funny, that was what I told the doctor. Almost verbatim. Apparently, it's not up to me."

"You don't understand."

"I assume it was that first time, in the castle before our wedding," she continued, her voice as falsely merry as her eyes were hard. "How romantic, I'm sure you'll agree. I took the liberty of paging through our contract this morning and it seems there's no provision for pregnancy—"

"Of course there isn't." Dimly, he understood that he was raging. That he'd shouted that. "I am the last of the Santa Dominis, Brittany. It ends with me. There cannot be another."

Her composure cracked at that, and all the things he'd tried so hard to ward off and keep at bay swept over him then as her hands crept over her flat belly. As her mouth softened, even trembled.

He had always been so careful. How had he let this happen?

"Cairo." He had never heard her so tentative, and that tore at him. "Is it really so bad?"

"Do you think I spent my wasted life in the tabloids for fun?" he threw at her. "I did it for protection. The more irredeemable I was, the less likely anyone would ever see me as a king. The moment I became anything like a king, the general would have me killed."

Brittany shook her head, her eyes flashing. "The general is dead."

She had to understand. She had to see the danger.

He closed the distance between them, wrapping his hands around her shoulders and putting his face in hers.

"I cannot have a child." He heard the thickness in his voice, the decades of grief and pain. "I cannot condemn an innocent to this life. I have never been a good man. I have never lived up to a single expectation. But I will not be that kind of monster, selfish beyond imagining. I will not lock a baby in this prison with me."

He didn't know when tears had begun to fall from her eyes, only that they tracked down her face. And the hands he'd put on her shoulders to keep her at a distance curved to hold her instead.

"You don't have to do this alone, Cairo," she whispered. "Don't you understand? You're not alone in this any longer."

"We have a plan—" he started.

"I love you," she said, very distinctly.

Again, the world was cleaved in two. And again, he could do nothing about it but mourn the split—and the inevitability of what he had to do.

"No," he said, very clearly, so she could not possibly mistake the matter. "You do not."

"Of course I love you." She scowled at him. "You're the only man I've ever let touch me. I not only let you touch me, I threw myself into it without a single thought about the consequences. Please. I know exactly where babies come from, Cairo. I knew about condoms before I knew my own telephone number. None of these things are accidents."

"None of those things matter," he said. He shook his head, trying to clear it. Trying to think. "We will have to fabricate a lover and have him claim the child. It will be a huge scandal. The baby you tried to pass off as mine—"

"No."

She didn't scowl. She didn't shout. She simply stood there, her hand curved over her belly, her face pale, as if she was carved from marble, and as movable.

"No?" he echoed.

"No," she said again, even more firmly. "This is your baby. I am your wife. I'm done playing these games, Cairo."

"You already agreed to play them."

"I agreed to play tabloid tag with a man who doesn't exist," she said, and though her voice was still thick with emotion, she didn't waver. "But then I fell in love with you. The real you. The man who, deep down when everything is stripped away, is a king. The true king of Santa Domini, no matter what happened in the interim."

"The true king of Santa Domini died in a car crash years ago." Cairo's voice was harsh with the past. Bitter. "I am nothing but his embarrassing shadow."

"The general stole your country. He killed your family. He forced you into this terrible game and, worse than that, somehow got you to believe that the act you put on is who you really are."

"It is no act. How else can I tell you?"

But he couldn't bring himself to drop his hands, to step away.

"Is that what you want for this baby?" she asked him softly, her dark hazel eyes hard and beseeching at once.

"You want to condemn him to the same game? The same lie of a life in public, until it starts to feel real in private, too?"

"You have no idea what you're talking about." But he dropped his gaze to that belly of hers. "You have no idea what is involved."

"Here's what I know." And Brittany pulled herself away from his grasp, stepping back so he had no choice but to let her go. He saw the sheen of emotion in her eyes and the resolve, too. "Neither one of us had any choice. We did what we had to do, and our lives played out in a hundred different tabloids because of it. But our child deserves better."

"I agree," he said fiercely. "That is why no one must know it's mine."

She drew herself up to her full height and there was no pretending she was anything but regal. She had been from the start.

"I won't run. I won't hide and I won't lie. I am your queen and this baby is the heir to your kingdom. Don't you understand?"

She searched his gaze and he didn't want to hide from it any longer. From her. When he knew she was the only one who'd ever really seen him in years.

The only one who had ever known the man he'd hidden beneath a series of masks, each more elaborate than the next.

"It doesn't matter if you love me," she told him, and his heart twisted in his chest at the quiet resolve in the way she said that. "What matters is the future. The future you never had, but your child can. The general is dead. It's *your* throne, Cairo. All you have to do is claim it."

CHAPTER TEN

THIRTY YEARS AFTER escaping it in the middle of the night, His Serene Grace the Archduke Felipe Skander Cairo of Santa Domini walked back into the Royal Palace that his family had held for generations.

It had been remarkably easy to retrace his family's steps. Up into the mountains and over the border, then down through the farthest villages, making his way through the very heart of the alpine kingdom he had been born to protect.

And with every step, he knew. That this was right. That this was home. That even if what was left of the general's military executed him the moment he set foot in the palace, this was where he belonged.

In his country, with his people, taking back what was his so that no child of his blood would be forced to live as he had done all these miserable years.

The white-covered mountains were deep in his bones. The green hills, the crystal-blue lakes—they pumped in his blood. They made him who he was.

By the time he reached the palace gates, he had attracted followers and the inevitable press. But he didn't stop to read headlines or gauge public sentiment.

He didn't care what the papers said. This was right. Finally, he was doing what was right.

Ricardo stood proud at his side. Hundreds of loyalists stood at his back. The police had met them outside the capital city, but rather than arresting them all, had only escorted the procession along their route toward the palace.

"You are a movement, Sire," Ricardo told him.

Cairo knew better. He was a man. He was a mediocre husband and he was already well on his way to being a terrible father. He was famous for all the wrong reasons and he'd squandered the better part of his life in fear.

But none of that mattered, because one woman had looked straight into the monster in him and seen only the king.

Today, at long last, he would claim that crown.

He walked through the palace gates that the general's remaining cronies didn't dare close against the rightful heir to the Santa Domini throne. Not when he had made this so public. He climbed the ceremonial steps, as aware of the news helicopters buzzing overhead as he was of the brave men and women who walked with him, ushering him toward his uncertain future.

But he would walk to meet it with his head held high. As his father would have wanted him to do, he knew without question.

He hadn't been in the palace since he was five years old, but Cairo knew his way. He marched past the ancient canvases that depicted his ancestors, the frescoes and the marbled halls, to the grand throne room that he knew full well had not been used since his father had last sat there thirty years ago.

That was where they met him, a pack of fat, old men with soft hands and shifty-eyed guards.

Cairo did not wait for them to speak.

"Good afternoon, gentlemen," he said, stopping halfway across the polished floors and standing there beneath the statue of his grandfather, aware that there were cameras on him, as there were always cameras on him. Today he was grateful for it.

And he was aware that no matter what happened here, he would be remembered for this moment above all others in his life.

Better make it good.

"I am Cairo, the last of the Santa Dominis. I believe you have been waiting to execute me for the crime of possessing my father's blood for the past thirty years." He inclined his head, though his eyes glittered and he felt his rage inside him like a drum. "Here I am. Do with me as you will."

Brittany watched the dramatic reclamation of the Santa Domini throne with the rest of the dumbstruck world—on television, hidden away in a safe house in one of Cairo's lesser known properties in the remote Scottish highlands.

It had been part of the bargain they'd struck when Cairo told her what he planned to do, and what he needed her to do if he did not live through it.

It hadn't been lost on her that Cairo had not expected to survive. But it was one more thing she couldn't allow herself to examine too closely.

She and a Hollywood actor as well known for his collection of children by assorted famous mothers as for any actual acting waited out the march into Santa Domini together in the drafty old manor house. Meaning she had watched it live on the twenty-four-hour news channel in the cozy den while the blandly attractive, deeply boring man in question had done push-ups in the gallery and spent several hours on his mobile phone shouting at his agent.

"You don't have to stay any longer," she'd told him after Cairo walked into the palace. When the remaining ministers resigned on the spot and the bells of all the Santa Domini churches began to ring out across the land after lying dormant for thirty years.

Long Live the King! the news sites and the people cheered.

As if Cairo had never been scandalous in all his life.

Because he was the king, she understood. She was his scandal.

"I don't understand why I was here for this," the actor told her, annoyed. "Why would anyone pay that much money to have me just…sit around for a week?"

"Rich people are strange," Brittany said coolly. "Royals are worse."

Then she'd dismissed him and waited for the car to take her to the plane that would deliver her to her own fate.

She landed in Santa Domini the following morning.

Aides whisked her from the plane into a fleet of gleaming black cars with tinted windows, hurrying her into the palace as if they were trying to hide her from the public. She imagined that was exactly what they were doing. It was exactly what she'd expected they'd do.

Cairo might have been instantly forgiven his scandalous past by virtue of his being, in fact, a king. But she was a girl who'd taken her clothes off for a living and then married a few men for obvious practical reasons. There was no forgiveness for her. Especially when the king himself didn't love her.

She told herself it didn't hurt, because it shouldn't. This wasn't about her or her feelings or her battered heart. It was about the baby that grew inside her daily. It was about a different sort of love altogether.

She told herself that had to be enough.

Brittany didn't see Cairo again until they led her out onto the balcony high above the palace's famous square, where kings had addressed the nation for centuries. She had been dressed and styled by a pack of palace attendants, then brought here to wait for him with everyone else.

He strode from the great doors and did nothing more

than slide a swift, intense look her way on his way to his podium. She made herself smile. Because what mattered was that he claimed his throne and took back his kingdom so that his child would never have to hide as he'd done.

She smiled dutifully in her lovely silver gown, her hair sleek and sophisticated, as if she really was a queen. And then watched the man she'd never meant to fall in love with, the father of the baby she carried within her, take his rightful place before his people.

It didn't matter that he didn't love her, that no one could or ever had. What mattered, she told herself as he stood there so proud and tall and beautiful, was that she loved him. She hadn't known she could. She'd worried she'd been broken by her family, her squalid, public life. But she loved him, and that was a good thing, regardless of what happened next.

"I have been hiding in plain sight the whole of my adult life," Cairo told the huge, cheering crowd, and all the world. "I believed I served my country by disappointing it, day after day. By rendering myself the least likely king, I ensured not only that I survived, but that the vile enemies of this kingdom could not vent their spleen on any who supported me."

He stood there in the same sort of suit he'd always worn, the very height of male elegance and every inch of him royal. He was the same man he'd always been, so beautiful it almost hurt to look at him. But now, Brittany knew, the whole world saw what she'd always seen beneath all of that. The real man within him, brave and true, who had always been more than the role he'd played.

The man she loved desperately and totally, with every fiber of her being, but could never truly have as she had during those stolen weeks on the island.

He was the King of Santa Domini.

She was a jumped up stripper whose own mother was ashamed of her antics.

His voice was sure and true as he addressed his subjects. Brittany called on all her years of pretending, all the acting she'd done and all the situations she'd had to weather, and stood there smiling as if her world wasn't ending right there in front of her.

The pain of it would pass. Or fade, anyway. She was sure it would, some day. She would always be his footnote. And the mother of his child.

But because she loved him, she would step aside as soon as she could do so without causing him any further scandal, and let him marry the sort of woman fit for a king.

It wouldn't make her child any less his heir, and that, she told herself firmly, was the only thing that mattered. That and the life the child could live, a life not on the run, a life that Cairo hadn't had.

Out there in front of her, Cairo was still speaking. He talked of his parents. He talked of his sister, the lost princess, Magdalena. He mourned the dead and promised that he would see to it that any citizen of the kingdom who had suffered under the general's rule would meet with him if they wished, so he could personally see to it that their suffering was ended.

Brittany thought she'd never seen a man better suited to be a king.

That was why, when her phone had rung beside her while she'd been getting ready earlier, flashing her mother's number and promising the usual punishment, she'd ignored it.

She didn't need that abuse anymore. She didn't need to feel badly about herself to know who she was.

She would survive this. She would do more than merely survive this. She loved a man who loved his country, and she wasn't afraid of the sacrifices ahead of her, no matter that they might prove difficult. Life was often difficult. That didn't mean it wasn't good.

For the first time since she'd left that island, and since she'd found out she was pregnant, Brittany felt at peace.

And Cairo was still speaking, his voice ringing out over those famous palace steps, down into the fairy-tale courtyard, and all across the world that had always hung on his every word, but never so much as today.

"Some have asked, why now? What prompted me to find my way back to my people, my country, my life?" He shifted, and glanced over his shoulder, his caramel gaze grazing hers. It was a swift, quick glance, and yet it was as if he looked straight into her soul. Brittany found she was holding her breath. "It was not the ignominious fall of a vicious man who fancied himself a dictator, let me assure you. It was something far less noble than the urge to do my duty. I found myself a woman who wasn't the least bit impressed with me and I made her my queen."

That statement went through her like a lightning bolt. And it hurt.

She'd imagined he'd issue a tasteful statement, released quietly sometime after the world had grown used to the return of the king. Not…here, now. With so many people as witnesses.

Brittany had to remind herself that the whole world was watching. That this was not for her or even about her. This was about a kingdom that deserved better than a stripper queen. Better than an infamous woman who had only ever learned how to make money and headlines. She reminded herself that Cairo was not hers. That he had never been hers, not really, no matter that she carried their baby inside of her or wore the Heart of Santa Domini on her hand.

He belonged to his people. He had only ever been on loan.

But she cradled the precious ring with the fingers of

her other hand anyway, as if she thought someone might come and try to take it from her right there where she stood. She would give it back when asked, of course. She would do the right thing.

Until then, she'd pretend this was the fairy tale that deep down she'd always dreamed about, no matter how many times life kicked her in the teeth instead.

She lifted her chin. In front of her, Cairo smiled, then turned back to his subjects and all those cameras.

Brittany braced herself. And she smiled.

"I made her my queen and she made me a man," Cairo told the world. "And as I learned to be the kind of man who deserved such a queen as Brittany, kind and true, strong and brave, I understood what I owed not only to her, but to you, the people of Santa Domini. I did not know if I would claim my throne or lose my life when I returned here. I only knew that I could not live with myself if I stayed in hiding, forever on the run, forever a man unworthy of both his queen and his country."

He lifted his arm and raised it toward the crowd. "I pledge to you that I will always strive to be the king you deserve, and to serve this country with every breath and bone in my body."

Then he turned.

King Cairo, resplendent and fierce in the clear mountain air, with thousands of adoring subjects cheering him on from below.

Today, Brittany knew exactly what that glorious mouth of his tasted like, and how it felt against every part of her skin. She knew the heavy silk of his dark hair and how it felt to run her hands through it. She missed the careless scruff he'd shaved from his astonishingly handsome face, the better to show off that perfectly cut Santa Domini jaw.

And, oh, his eyes. They were caramel and they were

wicked and they were focused on her as if there was nothing else in all the world but the two of them.

He held her gaze for a moment.

Then the rightful king of Santa Domini dropped to his knees before her. Her heart stopped. Then pounded into her, wild against her ribs, so hard she almost toppled over.

"Brittany," he said, as if they were alone, though the microphone on his lapel transmitted his words around the globe, "I love you."

The crowd roared. And Brittany didn't have it in her to fight the tears that spilled over and poured down her cheeks.

"No," she told him, because she had to. Because he deserved a real queen. A good one, who was proper and good and had never been featured in a burlesque ensemble in a tabloid—much less on a reality television program. "You can't. You're a king."

"And you are a queen," he replied, the maddening man. "My queen."

And Brittany forgot the crowds, the cameras. She forgot where they were. They might as well have been back on their own private island, with nothing for miles in all directions but the deep blue sea.

Cairo held out his hands, then waited.

Brittany pulled in a breath, then let it out. She needed to walk away. She knew she needed to walk away. She knew she didn't deserve to be here, with him. She was supposed to be the joke he played on the world. She couldn't stay with him and let him become the joke because of her…

But she couldn't bring herself to do it.

She didn't *want* to walk away from him.

So instead she reached out and took his hands, feeling the heat of his instant, sure grip go through her, warming her like the sun.

"You married an exiled royal with a terrible reputation," he said, his voice low and sure and his eyes on her. "And you made him into a king. You wear the Heart of Santa Domini on your hand and you hold my own heart between your palms. I want you to marry me again, in the cathedral where generations of Santa Dominis have pledged their lives to each other, so I can make you the queen in my people's eyes that you have always been to me."

She opened her mouth to refuse him. To sacrifice the very thing she wanted most, the only man she'd ever loved and the only person she'd ever let get close to her—but she looked into Cairo's warm, steady gaze, and she found she couldn't do it. Not to him, not to their baby.

Not to herself.

The truth was simple. She didn't want to live without him.

Maybe, just maybe, he wasn't crazy. Maybe they could do this.

She knew she had to try.

"If you think I can be the queen you need," she said, and heard her voice echo back at her from all over the vast palace complex and the Santa Domini mountains that surrounded them, "then I promise you, I will do my best to live up to that honor every day of my life. I promise."

Cairo's smile broke across his face, brighter than the summer's day around him. He surged to his feet and he pulled her into his arms, and the whole of his kingdom cheered for them, loud and long.

So loud and so long that nobody could hear him when he leaned in closer, his gaze hard and hot and hungry on hers, just the way she liked it.

"I love you," he told her again, this time for only her. "I will never let you go, *tesorina.* Never."

"You'd better not, Your Maddening Majesty," she said. Then smiled back at him, hope and love and the whole of their future dancing there between them. "Just think of the headlines."

"I always do," Cairo replied, arrogant and sure.

And entirely hers, forever.

Then he bent her back over his arms, a dashing king and his Cinderella queen, and kissed her like a fairy tale come true.

Because, Brittany knew with a rock-deep certainty, it finally had.

* * * * *

Don't miss Caitlin Crews's next story,
book 4 of THE BILLIONAIRE'S LEGACY *series*
THE RETURN OF THE DI SIONE WIFE.
Coming soon!

In the meantime,
don't miss Lynne Graham's 100th book!
BOUGHT FOR THE GREEK'S REVENGE.
Also available this month.

Lynne Graham has sold 35 million books!

To settle a debt, she'll have to become his mistress...

Nikolai Drakos is determined to have his revenge against the man who destroyed his sister. So stealing his enemy's intended fiancé seems like the perfect solution! Until Nikolai discovers that woman is Ella Davies…

Read on for a tantalising excerpt from Lynne Graham's 100th book,

BOUGHT FOR THE GREEK'S REVENGE

Mistress,' Nikolai slotted in cool as ice.

Shock had welded Ella's tongue to the roof of her mouth because he was sexually propositioning her and nothing could have prepared her for that. She wasn't drop-dead gorgeous… *he* was! Male heads didn't swivel when Ella walked down the street because she had neither the length of leg nor the curves usually deemed necessary to attract such attention. Why on earth could he be making *her* such an offer?

'But we don't even know each other,' she framed dazedly. 'You're a stranger…'

'If you live with me I won't be a stranger for long,' Nikolai pointe out with monumental calm. And the very sound of that inhuma calm and cool forced her to flip round and settle distraught eye on his lean darkly handsome face.

'You can't be serious about this!'

'I assure you that I am deadly serious. Move in and I'll forge your family's debts.'

'But it's a *crazy* idea!' she gasped.

'It's not crazy to me,' Nikolai asserted. 'When I want anything, go after it hard and fast.'

Her lashes dipped. Did he want her like that? Enough to trac her down, buy up her father's debts, and try and buy rights to he and her body along with those debts? The very idea of that mad her dizzy and plunged her brain into even greater turmoil. 'It' immoral... it's blackmail.'

'It's definitely *not* blackmail. I'm giving you the benefit of a choic you didn't have before I came through that door,' Nikolai Drako fielded with a glittering cool. 'That choice is yours to make.'

'Like hell it is!' Ella fired back. 'It's a complete cheat of a suppose offer!'

Nikolai sent her a gleaming sideways glance. 'No the real chea was you kissing me the way you did last year and then saying n and acting as if I had grossly insulted you,' he murmured with letha quietness.

'You *did* insult me!' Ella flung back, her cheeks hot as fire whil she wondered if her refusal that night had started off his whole chai reaction. What else could possibly be driving him?

Nikolai straightened lazily as he opened the door. 'If you tak offence that easily, maybe it's just as well that the answer is no.'